'We don't hav

It's just impossibl
that!'

'Why's it impossible?' She leaned closer as she asked the question and he could see down the front of her shirt to the deep cleft between her breasts. Desire tightened his body again, while frustration blew the lid off his temper.

'Because there are too many question marks hanging over my head,' he roared. 'I thought I could sort out the past—put it behind me. It's why I wanted time off—to finalise things once and for all. Then I could... Perhaps we could...'

As his voice trailed away Rowena felt her heart jerk. Was he saying he *did* feel something for her?

'So what's different now?' she asked, although she already knew the answer.

'Mary-Ellen's arrival!' David replied. 'She hasn't come to wish me well in my future, Rowena. She's come to stir up trouble.'

DR DETECTIVE—DOWN UNDER

Meet Australian GP Dr Sarah Kemp
(if you haven't done already)—a lady
who is no stranger to the world of forensic medicine.

In this intriguing series from Australian author
Meredith Webber discover how her heroes and
heroines struggle to find romance against all the
odds—amidst intrigue, mayhem—and even murder!

The next book in
DR DETECTIVE—DOWN UNDER

A Woman Worth Waiting For
coming soon in April 2002.

Other books by the same author in the
DR DETECTIVE—DOWN UNDER miniseries:

TRUST ME
LOVE ME
MARRY ME

HER DR WRIGHT

BY
MEREDITH WEBBER

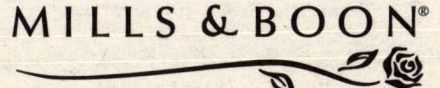

DID YOU PURCHASE THIS BOOK WITHOUT A COVER?

If you did, you should be aware it is **stolen property** as it was reported *unsold and destroyed* by a retailer. Neither the author nor the publisher has received any payment for this book.

All the characters in this book have no existence outside the imagination of the author, and have no relation whatsoever to anyone bearing the same name or names. They are not even distantly inspired by any individual known or unknown to the author, and all the incidents are pure invention.

All Rights Reserved including the right of reproduction in whole or in part in any form. This edition is published by arrangement with Harlequin Enterprises II B.V. The text of this publication or any part thereof may not be reproduced or transmitted in any form or by any means, electronic or mechanical, including photocopying, recording, storage in an information retrieval system, or otherwise, without the written permission of the publisher.

This book is sold subject to the condition that it shall not, by way of trade or otherwise, be lent, resold, hired out or otherwise circulated without the prior consent of the publisher in any form of binding or cover other than that in which it is published and without a similar condition including this condition being imposed on the subsequent purchaser.

MILLS & BOON and MILLS & BOON with the Rose Device are registered trademarks of the publisher.

*First published in Great Britain 2002
Harlequin Mills & Boon Limited,
Eton House, 18-24 Paradise Road, Richmond, Surrey TW9 1SR*

© Meredith Webber 2002

ISBN 0 263 83053 5

*Set in Times Roman 10½ on 11¼ pt.
03-0302-51788*

*Printed and bound in Spain
by Litografía Rosés, S.A., Barcelona*

PROLOGUE

'MUCH as I'd love to, David, I don't know that I can—I've a family to consider these days.'

Sarah Kemp pressed the receiver to her ear, listening to David Wright's rush of understanding and apology, while, across the room, her husband was mouthing words at her and waving his arms in the air. Though how anyone could make sense of his whispered questions and strange gesticulations...

'Tell him you'll call him back!' Tony suggested, obviously frustrated by his attempts to get his message across with hand signals.

'David, can I talk to Tony about this and call you back?'

Another rush of words, of agreement this time. David *must* be in a tizz over his impending holiday for him to be talking so much. She asked for his number to save the bother of searching outdated address books for it, and promised to call back in an hour.

'Was that your friend David from Three Ships Island?' Tony demanded, as soon as she was off the phone. 'Did he want you to do a locum? Wouldn't you like to do it? Haven't you been saying you must get back to proper work before you forget what it's all about? Why did you hesitate?'

Sarah smiled at her husband. Since the arrival of James, twelve months ago, she'd worked occasional days at the local health service, and though, from time to time, she'd missed the closer association with colleagues and patients which her locum work had brought her, she had no regrets about the time she'd spent at home with their baby.

Tony, however, had worried about it, thinking it a sacrifice on her part.

'Yes, and yes, and yes,' she told him, answering his questions one by one. 'And why did I hesitate? Because it's so far away and I don't want to be separated from you and James for any length of time.'

'But I've always wanted to go there!' Tony protested, in the tone of someone being denied a treat. 'You wouldn't have to be away from us. I've leave due to me, and even if I can't go immediately, Lucy arrives tomorrow. I bet she'd be happy to mind the brat until I can get away—then James and I will fly over and join you. Lucy, too, if she wants to come. Nowhere's too far away these days!'

Sarah considered the implications of a family holiday on a small and isolated island off the southern coast of Australia. Lucy, her much-loved daughter from a previous relationship, would soon be home from university. It was as though fate had decreed that various pieces of the past should now come together, as it was David, who had been Lucy's father's best friend, who was now appealing to her for help.

David Wright put down the phone and looked out the window to where a wind-tossed sea beyond the headland reminded him of the difficulties inherent in living and working on an island.

Of course Sarah hadn't wanted to come! Not long married, and with a toddler to consider, it had been a foolish idea in the first place.

But she understood small communities, and also the delicate balancing act good locum work required—convincing patients one was capable without in any way diminishing the efforts of the absent doctor. She was the ideal choice because he hadn't spent three years getting the locals to accept him, only to ruin things with one bad locum.

'Problem?'

Rowena Jackman walked into the room, stopping on the far side of his desk.

He swung back to face her and felt the now familiar surge of desire her presence generated these days. Though why, after three years of working with this nurse-receptionist, he was suddenly seeing her as a woman—lusting after her as a woman—was a mystery.

Or perhaps it was a sign he was finally over the trauma of Sue-Ellen's disappearance—and the hell that had followed it!

'Sarah's calling back,' he said, hoping his voice sounded more noncommittal than he felt. Since realising how he felt about Rowena, his sole aim had been to put away the past for ever—and having Sarah here would give him the time to make it possible.

Rowena smiled, then said with the gentle firmness he'd come to know so well, 'Well if she can't do it, you'll just have to get someone who can. You've had three years without a holiday that I know of—heaven only knows how long you went before you came here!'

Six years in all, he could have told her. He'd not had a real break since his honeymoon. Unless you counted a snatched few days here and there, and a tactfully suggested period of 'stress leave' from his group practice while he'd been investigated for murder.

He hid the shudder of reaction that particular thought caused—though the memories of his honeymoon were just as bad. Skiing at Aspen had sounded great in theory, until he'd discovered his new bride had had no intention of hitting the slopes. Her idea of a skiing holiday had been ensuring she didn't miss any of the A-list social events being held at the time.

He focussed on Rowena to chase away the memories, and seeing her—her blonde hair coiled loosely on her neck, her skin lightly tanned from the long walks she took in her free time, her dark-lashed grey eyes steadfast and concerned—he felt more than desire.

Perhaps love?

'If Sarah can't come, I'll try an agency,' he told her, then he smiled to reassure her because he could feel her anxiety clear across the room. 'I'll take this holiday, I promise you!'

An inner smile accompanied the promise, starting a warmth in places cold for too long.

'You'd better,' she threatened, then turned the conversation to the patient list for the day.

And though he listened to the words, and nodded to show he was following, the warmth inside him flickered into something like excitement. What would Rowena think if she knew exactly why he was so determined?

And how, when he'd sorted out the past and shut it away for ever, would she react to his declaration of—well, interest, he supposed was how you put it? But interest was such a feeble word for how he was beginning to feel about Rowena.

CHAPTER ONE

'So, WHERE are you going for this long-awaited holiday?' Sarah asked, when, after a day and a half of introduction, she was about to be left in charge of David's practice.

'Would you believe Three Ships Island?' he said, grinning at her with such delight he reminded her of the fun-loving student she'd known so long ago—before life had dealt him a series of cruel and bitter blows.

'You're s-staying here?' she stuttered. 'On the island? Why? Don't you trust me to take care of your patients?'

His smile grew broader, lightening the dark brown eyes with sparks of suppressed excitement. But all he said was, 'I have my reasons!'

One of which, Sarah guessed, having sussed out the atmosphere in less than two days, was a certain nurse-receptionist in the outer office—the lovely Rowena Jackman.

Though *she* wasn't taking holidays...

'OK—be mysterious!' Sarah told him. 'See if I care.'

David chuckled.

'Of course you care. It's why you're such a great locum. You throw yourself into things with such gusto. You love people, and it shows. In fact, you'll probably learn more about my patients in a month than I've learnt in three years.'

Well, hopefully I'll learn more about Rowena, Sarah thought, though she turned the conversation back to medical matters, discussing the extent of her duties at the small hospital across the road from the surgery—a facility staffed by a group of full- and part-time nurses and some ancillary staff.

'Any patient with major medical needs is airlifted to the mainland,' David reminded her.

'What about the weather? Can that be a problem with arranging air transport?'

David smiled.

'Of course, but it doesn't affect us too often,' he assured her. 'They're hardy folk, the islanders, used to making do when the weather turns bad—which it can for weeks on end. Though at this time of the year, with storms likely, there aren't many tourists, so you don't get many accident victims, who are the most likely to require air evacuation.'

'Well, I hope the weather doesn't turn bad for a few days at least—Tony, Lucy and James are flying over on Friday's flight.'

'I saw a long-range forecast last night and though there's a front approaching, it's slow moving, so the flight should come in,' David assured her. 'But if it doesn't, there's always Monday's flight, the one you came on, or, as a last resort, the ferry next Tuesday. It takes a really wild storm to stop the *Trusty*.'

'An aptly named boat!' Sarah responded, then she lifted a pile of forms and assorted paperwork off the desk and held it towards David.

'Do you want me to tackle some of this in my spare time? From what I've heard and seen so far, I'm not going to be rushed off my feet with customers.'

'If you wouldn't mind,' David replied. 'I know I should have had it done before I left, but the tourist season was busier than usual and then we had the bush fires, which meant when I wasn't doctoring injured fire-fighters, or tending native animals, I was fighting fires or shifting stock myself. The first of the winter storms, the week before I phoned you, was very welcome.'

It was also when he'd realised just how deep his feelings for Rowena went—not only working with her at the surgery, but seeing her beside him as he'd battled flames or hunted terrified sheep across already blackened pastures. Revelling in her refusal to be flustered by even the most hairy of situations, delighting in her uninhibited shouts of joy as the rain had finally come tumbling down!

'But you don't *have* to do it,' he added to Sarah, trying to blot out an image of a very wet and surprisingly sexy Rowena with work-related thoughts. 'Most of it is non-urgent and can wait until I come back.'

When, hopefully, my head will be clear, my past laid to rest and I could possibly have an exciting future ahead of me.

There was a tap at the door and Rowena popped her head in—right on cue.

But Rowena's clear eyes were filled with pain, and her lips trembled uncertainly as she said, 'There's a woman here to see you, David. She said you'd be expecting her.'

Beyond Rowena, backlit by the light of the setting sun beyond the open door of the surgery, stood his long-lost wife.

His heart kicked so hard against his ribs he felt his throat close and he wondered briefly if shock could kill a man who was otherwise healthy. Then rational thought returned. It would be Mary-Ellen, not Sue, though why she'd think he was expecting her...

Rowena had seen the colour leach from his cheeks, and she stepped closer, gripping his arm, offering support in the only way she knew, by being close to him.

'It's *Mary*-Ellen,' she whispered fiercely. 'It *has* to be.'

She was far from certain, but David's sanity depended on the woman in the waiting room *not* being his wife. He'd already been through the whole dreadful process of grief and denial and hurt and anger, not to mention dealing with the accusations and suspicion, when his wife had disappeared. Now he was finally coming out the other end.

For Sue-Ellen to reappear—to reclaim him—would be too much!

Wouldn't it?

'You didn't have to come,' David stuttered, brushing Rowena aside, as if she didn't exist, to tower over the diminutive newcomer. 'I told you I'd draw up an inventory for you, then whatever you wanted to keep, I'd have packed and shipped on to you.'

The ebony-haired woman, with her perfect features and classically casual elegance, stood her ground.

'So you'd inventory *everything*, would you?' she demanded. 'Or only the things you didn't fancy keeping for yourself?'

Rowena saw David's shoulders tense, and longed to go to him, but he'd already brushed her off once. Her heart ached with the frustration of a love she couldn't reveal, and the agony of not being able to comfort him.

Sarah had seen her friend go deathly pale and, looking beyond where Rowena had been murmuring something to him, had understood why. She'd never met Sue-Ellen Wright but photos splashed across the paper at the time of her disappearance had shown a petite but beautiful redhead, with perfect features and a look of polish that shrieked of wealth and privilege.

The woman in the waiting room might have dark hair, but the same precise features seemed untouched by age, and the air of assurance was more obvious than any photo could indicate.

Sarah replayed the initial scene in her head. David had been shocked by this woman's arrival but he certainly didn't seem surprised to find his missing wife alive and well and standing in his waiting room.

Less tactful than Rowena, who'd retreated further into the office, Sarah cocked her head to listen to the conversation.

'I'd prefer to go through the things with you,' the visitor was saying. 'I assume I can stay in my sister's house?'

Sister? It was the twin! Light dawned in Sarah's brain,

but Rowena must have missed the conversation and was still confused. In fact, she looked downright ill, leaning back against the filing cabinet, her pale eyes vivid against even paler skin.

'Come here and sit down,' Sarah murmured to her. 'We'll shut the door and let them work things out in peace. Do you know who she is?'

'One of them! Of the twins,' Rowena muttered bitterly. 'Presumably his sister-in-law, though who would know? It could just as easily be Sue-Ellen, risen from the dead or back from wherever she went, here to reclaim her man. They came to the island every Christmas for their holidays, and used to tease us local kids about how stupid we were. Said it was because we were all inbred. They played us for fools by swapping around so you never knew who was who! I can't understand how David ever...'

Rowena, perhaps realising she was saying too much, slumped into the patient's chair in front of David's desk and leant forward, resting the heels of her hands against her eyes.

'Hasn't he been tortured enough,' she muttered, 'without her turning up again? Just when he seemed to be getting over it—to be coming out from behind his frozen armour of pain and indifference—this has to happen. Though if he loves her, I guess...'

'It *is* his wife's sister,' Sarah assured the stricken woman. 'I heard her talk about her sister's house.'

She gave Rowena a comforting pat on the shoulder, and crossed the room to shut the door. David was still facing his sister-in-law, and the bunched fists he rammed into his pockets matched the lines of tension in his back.

Little love lost there!

'This is my friend, Paul,' the beautiful stranger added. 'He'll be staying at the house as well.'

Sarah saw the man step forward, wary watchfulness in every movement. She might only have been married to

Tony for a couple of years, but she could recognise one of his colleagues when she saw one. The man might as well have had POLICEMAN on a banner across his chest, although his attire, excellent quality casual gear, suggested he'd left the force and was doing something more financially rewarding.

Not that it was any of her business.

She was closing the door when David must have sensed her presence for, just as it was almost shut, she felt resistance and he pushed it open again.

'I'm sorry,' he said, addressing the woman, not Sarah. 'But I really won't have room to put you up. Most of the house has been closed for years and Sarah, my locum, is using the only habitable spare room. One of the things I was hoping to achieve with this time off was to clean out the rest of the house and decide if I want to sell it, or if I'm going to stay here.'

He ignored Sarah's start of surprise, and his visitor's hiss of anger, fixing her with a glare that challenged her to argue, as he added, 'After all, it is *my* house, and has been since I bought it from your grandfather's estate when Sue-Ellen and I were first married.'

The look the woman shot him in return should have singed his eyebrows, but David stood his ground, earning a silent cheer from Sarah. Although now he'd embroiled her and Tony in his battle with this uppity in-law. Not a good start to a restful holiday for Tony and Lucy, but James would love the animals David seemed to collect.

And they could all do their sightseeing from there.

She finished closing the door and leant against it, but it wasn't soundproof. She could hear the ongoing murmur of David's voice as he began listing the accommodation options on the island at this time of the year.

Rowena looked across at Sarah, her usually clear grey eyes bleak with confusion.

'I've loved him almost since the day he arrived,' she

admitted, speaking slowly as if this abrupt confession was being torn from her lips against her will. 'Only I didn't recognise it for a long time. I don't know why—why I loved him, not why I didn't know I did. Perhaps it was because he was so hurt and I'd been there myself and understood. It was as if we were the same under the skin.'

She rubbed the fingers of her right hand against her temple. 'I don't know why I'm telling you this when I've not even wanted to think about my feelings up till now.'

Sarah stayed where she was, fearing that movement might break the mood, but tried to transmit the empathy she was feeling across the room.

'Perhaps you need to put it into words to clarify your feelings,' she murmured.

Rowena nodded slowly, then continued her confession. 'Recently I've thought he might be beginning to see me differently—as more than just his colleague. Things he's said—the way he looks at me sometimes—but I haven't wanted to make a fool of myself...'

Her voice trailed away but Sarah knew exactly what Rowena meant. Love might be all-powerful, but there was so much uncertainty in the early stages of a relationship that walking through quicksand would be easy by comparison. While the pain of that uncertainty was immeasurable and seemingly infinite.

But now wasn't the right time for an in-depth discussion on relationships, so she picked up on something else Rowena had said.

'You've been there yourself? Suffered that kind of pain? I've seen the photo on your desk—your husband and son?'

Rowena nodded.

'It's five years now. My husband was the doctor here—we were both island bred, had grown up together. We went to the mainland to study, married young and had Adrian, then came back to work together at Three Ships. It had always been our dream. They went sailing one day, Peter and Adrian. He was five. The wind came up. Peter had sailed all his life. I assumed they'd taken shelter somewhere and would be back as soon as the wind dropped.'

She paused and rubbed her hand across her eyes as if to press back pain, and Sarah felt remnants of her own devastating loss so many years ago when Lucy's father had died in a car accident a week before their wedding—seven months before their daughter was born.

'It was not knowing what had happened!' Rowena continued. 'It nearly drove me crazy. So, when David decided to give up paediatrics and came to work here, though it was two years later, I understood what he was going through— or part of it. The dreadful uncertainty part. The loss and grief.'

She shrugged her shoulders. 'Though no one has ever accused me of murder! I've never been investigated. That's another whole issue David's had to deal with.'

'Had you known David before that? When he was married to Sue-Ellen?'

Rowena looked surprised by the question.

'Not really, though, of course, we knew of him from when he first met Sue-Ellen because her family were well known on the island and she and Mary-Ellen had always holidayed here. During their marriage, they spent occasional weekends here, but we didn't see them socially. Of course, when his wife disappeared...'

The sentence dropped away as if that time was too confusing to consider, then Rowena frowned and finished what she'd been saying before Sarah had interrupted.

'Anyway, when he came to work here, keeping Peter's dream of a doctor on the island alive, I came to help—the way I'd always intended.'

The words were so harshly defiant that Sarah looked down at her forearms to see if they'd scored her skin. No wonder these two had taken so long to come even close to getting together. Both of them, like she herself at one stage of her life, had been unwilling to commit to a new relationship and subject themselves to the possibility of even more pain. Neither of them had wanted to be overtaken by the vulnerability love imposed.

But love had apparently found, or was finding, a way through the maze, until a new problem, small in size but huge in its implications, now flared like a rocket across their path.

Effectively blocking all chance of a future for them?

Sarah hoped not. Though she hadn't known Rowena long, she suspected that this woman was the right one for David—a woman who could restore the gleam to his eyes and laughter to his voice.

A woman who could give him the happiness she and Tony shared.

Before she could tentatively suggest this might be possible, the door opened and David returned. His dark hair was tousled where he'd run his hand through it, and his face lined and drawn.

'Sarah!' He strode forward and took Sarah's hands in his. 'That was unforgivable of me to thrust you into such an unpleasant situation. But the thought of her staying there, in the house, knowing what she thinks of me...' He hesitated, raising tortured eyes to meet Sarah's. 'I took the easy way out, used you as an excuse. I'm sorry. Of course, there's no reason for you all to stay out at my place when your family arrives, though I've plenty of rooms—they just need cleaning out and I was intending to do that anyway. You can go back to the guest-house as we'd originally planned, if you'd prefer. I'll simply tell Mary-Ellen you changed your mind.'

Sarah squeezed his fingers.

'Nonsense! We'll be delighted to stay with you, as long as you let Tony and Lucy share the cooking and tell us when we're in your way. In fact, I was wondering how to ask you about alternative accommodation. The guest-house is lovely, so beautifully set up with its period furnishings and little knick-knacks, but I'm afraid James would wreak havoc there in ten minutes and Lucy's sleeping habits wouldn't fit with Lorelle's idea of mealtimes.'

She sensed David's relief.

'I'll explain to Lorelle,' he offered. 'And pay her for the time you'd have been there. Could you...? Would you mind...?'

'Shifting tonight?' Sarah rescued him. 'Not at all! I haven't unpacked much because I knew a house or flat would be better once the others arrived.'

David threw her a grateful smile, but the concern returned to his eyes when he looked towards the other occupant of his office.

'Rowena...' he began, hesitancy fudging his usually clear voice. 'I—'

Before he could finish, the statuesque blonde rose smoothly to her feet. She stepped towards him and looked him in the eyes.

'You know where I live, and how to contact me at any time,' she said bluntly. 'If there's anything I can do, and I mean *anything*, David, you have only to ask.'

Simple words but they produced a buzz of electric tension in the room. Sarah wished she could render herself invisible, for it was obviously a moment when David might have reached out to the woman who loved him.

Maybe admitted his own feelings...

But David, for all the notice he took, might not have heard. He'd certainly missed the emotion quivering in Rowena's voice. He turned away, his face closed, his lips tightening grimly, then a smile that didn't reach his eyes quirked the left side of his mouth upward just a little.

'I don't suppose that offer would extend to shooting my sister-in-law?' he said.

'Don't tempt me!' Rowena retorted as she left the room.

* * *

'For an island of two thousand souls, the actual towns, if you can call them that, are very small. It's always been primarily farming land, with some fishing and kelp-gathering in the season.'

They were heading out of the main settlement of Winship, after collecting Sarah's suitcase and appeasing the guest-house owner with a wad of cash. Now David seemed determined to act as a tour guide, probably to keep his mind off his other problems. Whatever worked, Sarah thought, and she sat back, content to listen, though most of what he was saying he'd already told her the day he'd picked her up from the airport.

'The fishing fleet uses Makepeace Harbour—presumably because they need to make peace with the elements before leaving home. It's about twenty kilometres east along the coast at the end of a long narrow inlet. The only other settlement of any size is Redwing, which is just about dead centre of the island. The farm is equidistant to all three places, so it was convenient for me to live there rather than in one of the towns.'

'Oh, look at the goats. Aren't they sweet?'

The sudden appearance, in the middle of the road, of the herd of long-haired, doe-eyed animals saved her asking the question that had curled on her tongue. The one about why, when this place was so intricately connected to memories of his wife, he had chosen to come here to work.

Not to mention giving up a lucrative paediatric practice to administer to the general health and well-being of his two thousand scattered souls.

'They're not goats but a weird breed of sheep, kept especially for their milk which is used to make a very tasty yoghurt—in fact, you've probably been eating it for breakfast at Lorelle's. Rowena's family, the Andersons, own that herd. The lad driving them across the road at peak hour is her nephew, Bart.'

She heard a softness in his voice when he mentioned

Rowena, but when Sarah glanced towards him his profile was just as grim as it had been since they'd left the surgery.

'Bart comes over quite often. He feeds my animals if I'm not able to get home for any reason.'

Talk of his animals—which apparently included a variety of native marsupials recovering from various injuries, plus one obstreperous ram, a confused pig, a couple of goats and a donkey—occupied the rest of the drive, although the questions she hadn't asked still nagged in Sarah's head. When she'd first learned of David's decision to become a GP on Three Ships, she'd assumed he'd wanted to cling to the ties with his lost wife.

Today's reaction to his sister-in-law's arrival, and a few earlier snippets of conversation they'd had, now had her wondering if the memories were all that happy.

Rowena stood at the surgery window and watched the two doctors depart. She envied Sarah her privileged position as 'old friend' in David's life. Envied the fact that she'd be the one closest to him at the moment, when he needed someone to lean on.

'You should be grateful he's got someone staying with him,' she told herself, but she wasn't. She was edgy and unhappy and probably, if she analysed the multitude of emotions surging in her body, a little jealous.

'Damn this for a joke!' she added, scowling at her hazy reflection in the darkening glass. 'And be damned to convention. Get off your butt, Rowena Jackman, and damn well fight for your man!'

The words echoed around the room, making her smile at the repetitive nature of her curses. Maybe it was time she began to use a few stronger ones.

The smile lingered on her lips as she locked the surgery and walked up the little back lane to her home. It hovered in her heart as she chopped meat and peeled vegetables. It warmed her as the casserole began to cook, and made her fingers fumble as she packed a small suitcase.

She showered, careful to keep her hair dry, then wrapped herself in a towel while she brushed the long tresses before pulling the whole swathe of it forward over her right shoulder and plaiting it loosely. The clothes she'd chosen for stage one of her campaign were laid out on the bed. Jeans—one wore little else on the island—and a rich purple linen shirt, with a bulky, hand-knitted cardigan for warmth.

Courtesy of one of the many clever craftswomen on the island, she had a well-padded cloth bag ideal for carrying a piping hot casserole, and with it in one hand and her suitcase in the other, she walked out to the car. It wasn't until she was driving down the lane that she realised she hadn't locked the house. Not that anyone locked up on the island—except when they were going away for any length of time.

She stopped the car very deliberately, walked back to the house, found the key after a flustered search and locked the house.

CHAPTER TWO

DAVID heard the car pull up as he was pouring Sarah a glass of wine. They'd put off the question of where she'd sleep until later, simply dumping her case and smaller bags in the hall before going outside to tend the animals while it was still light. She'd walked around with him, hovering, he had no doubt, in case he needed her support.

Though he wasn't going to fall to pieces just because Mary-Ellen had arrived. He'd been shocked, of course, particularly in the instant when he'd seen her as Sue-Ellen.

Seen his missing wife standing in the waiting room!

But he'd got over that and now he was going to take the next step towards burying the past. Starting tomorrow, no doubt with Mary-Ellen watching every move, he was going to sort through the huge shed filled with antique farm machinery, old horse-drawn vehicles and an assorted accumulation of generations of junk, and get rid of the lot, either to Mary-Ellen or a dealer.

It was time to start afresh!

The sound of the car—it was sure to be Mary-Ellen checking that Sarah *was* staying here—shook this resolve slightly. He stiffened his backbone and prepared to stand his ground. Politeness would prevent him from telling her exactly what he thought of her, but he'd not let her needle him or get to him in any way.

He passed Sarah the glass, and resisted reaching for a beer for himself as he heard the footsteps cross his veranda.

'Can I come in?'

His heart thudded—probably with relief, he told himself—as he recognised Rowena's voice, then the sound of her footsteps coming closer down the hall.

Funny how familiar those footsteps were—how natural-sounding in his hall.

'I'm bringing dinner so I was reasonably certain you wouldn't turn me away,' she added, coming into the light so he could tell from a wariness in her lovely eyes that she was far less certain than she was making out.

He could also see the suitcase.

'Leaving town?' Sarah asked.

Rowena dropped the case but retained her grip on the cloth bundle in her other hand.

'Yes, but not the island,' she said firmly. Then she turned to David. 'I've come to stay!'

'You can't!' he said, his voice deepening with denial in case she didn't understand the words. 'Not now!'

'Nonsense!' Rowena retorted. 'You just try to stop me. Now is exactly when you need friends around you and while I know you've got Sarah, she's not a local. You need local support as well, and that's me, David Wright, so get it into your thick head.'

'No!' he repeated, struggling to find the words he needed to make her understand. But while she stood before him, strong and straight, her eyes glittering with stubborn determination, he couldn't think at all.

Well, not rationally.

Irrationally, he wanted to kiss her—to hold her in his arms and lean his body into hers, feel her full breasts against his chest, the hardness of her pubic bone pressed into his groin...

'You can't,' he muttered weakly, then he turned to Sarah. 'You explain!'

'I don't see any reason why Rowena can't join us,' Sarah said, betraying their years of friendship without so much as a quiver of regret.

The anger which had churned beneath his apprehension

since setting eyes on Mary-Ellen now bubbled to the surface and was fuelled by his totally inappropriate but still frustrated lust.

'You must see why she can't stay,' he stormed at Sarah. 'With Mary-Ellen here, the entire unsavoury mess will be dug up again, and the whole island will be talking. I don't want Rowena involved in it—I don't want her hurt by the talk and gossip that will spread around the place faster than the summer bush fires. She's one of them, an islander. She belongs here and I won't have her contaminated by the filth that woman flung at me four years ago.'

'Then tell her so yourself,' Sarah told him, standing up the better to glare at him. 'Stop shilly-shallying around the place and tell the woman how you feel about her.'

The words hit David with all the impact of a force-ten gale!

'How I f-feel about her?' he stuttered, wondering how the devil Sarah had discovered his secret—almost before he'd figured things out himself.

Now his infuriating old friend was smiling at him, the kind of smug grin women used when hugging secrets to themselves! He scowled at her but it had little effect. The smile remained.

'As you two are discussing me as if I'm not here, I think I'll put the casserole in the oven,' Rowena said, but when she walked out of the room it felt colder.

'Well, you do fancy her, don't you?' Sarah persisted, the determination in her voice telling him she wasn't going to drop the subject.

'I don't quite know what I feel for her,' he prevaricated. 'But I do know I can't tell her anything—can't even think about courting her—until I've got rid of all the remnants of the past and can start afresh. Until I can offer her a whole man!'

Sarah chuckled.

'Courting! What a delightfully old-fashioned word it is!'

Then she reached out and touched him lightly on the shoulder.

'But old-fashioned or not, you've never been less than a whole man to any of us who love you,' she said. 'A hurt man, certainly. A man who felt lost, bewildered and betrayed. But never less than whole, David.'

She kissed him gently on the cheek then she, too, left the room. Presumably to find Rowena.

David closed his eyes as the name echoed in his head.

Rowena!

And she'd come to stay!

The warmth and excitement he'd been denying for months threatened to burn right through him, until another echo—this time of the final words—sounded in his head.

Come to stay?

When all he had were two habitable bedrooms and Sarah—soon to be Sarah and her family—would need more than that for themselves.

He strode towards the kitchen where both women were perched on the edge of the table, their legs stretched out towards the warmth of the Aga, seemingly at ease in spite of the threat of catastrophe hovering over all their heads.

'You can't stay here—there's no room!' he said to Rowena.

'When I was growing up this house had eight bedrooms. What have you done with them all? Rented them out to ghosts? Turned them into dens for your animals?'

'No, but they've not been opened for years. There are beds in most of them, but who knows what state they're in? There'll be inches of dust, ash from the fires and probably mice—certainly spiders...'

Rowena didn't answer him, turning instead to Sarah and smiling as she said, 'Do you think he's trying to put me off?'

'Sounds like it,' Sarah responded, her lips twitching in enjoyment of this womanly conspiracy. 'Mind you, there's always David's bed. I checked it out when he was leading me through the house earlier and it looked clean enough. It also seemed, in that quick glance, to be free of mice and spiders.'

At least Rowena had the grace to blush at Sarah's suggestion, while David was choking on it—probably to death!

'Will you keep your nose out of other people's business?' he yelled, then realised he'd missed the point and blundered on. 'The last thing Rowena wants is to share my bed!'

Sarah grinned at his confusion.

'Oh, I wouldn't be too sure about that!' she said, then added with infuriating composure, 'Though who said anything about sharing your bed? Was it something you had on your mind, David, darling?'

She waltzed out of the room, pausing in the doorway long enough to offer some feeble excuse about phoning home.

'I thought she phoned Tony earlier,' David grumbled, when embarrassment forced him to break the silence Sarah had left in her wake.

'I guess if she phones again now, she can say goodnight to James before he goes to bed.'

Rowena's words made perfect sense but they meant nothing to David. He was too busy trying to sort out the bed situation—wondering what to say to Rowena, how to counteract Sarah's ridiculous suggestion without hurting Rowena in the process.

The very last thing he wanted was for her to think he was rejecting her.

'The potatoes must be nearly done,' she said, and he was so grateful to her for taking the initiative to end the silence this time that he smiled at her.

'I'll set the table. And would you like a glass of wine? I opened a bottle for Sarah—you'll share it?'

He muddled through the courtesies, his heart thudding

with anxiety and his mouth as woolly as fleece, though it wasn't the first time Rowena had eaten in this house. While the fires had been raging close by, they'd often popped in for a snack. But Sarah's comment had shifted the parameters of their relationship.

No! Rowena's arrival had shifted them.

What did it mean?

Was it simply, as she'd said, to provide local support?

In which case, Sarah's foolish comments must have embarrassed her no end.

He walked back into the living room to fetch the wine, more confused than he'd been for years. The excitement he felt in Rowena's presence was like his first adolescent longing for a shapely fellow high-school student—and his behaviour as blunderingly pathetic now as it had been then.

Perhaps if he sorted out priorities…

'I would hate to see you hurt in any way!' he said, returning to the kitchen a little later and handing Rowena a glass of wine. 'You've already suffered more than your share of pain.'

Rowena raised her glass to him and smiled.

'No pain without gain—isn't that the saying?'

He felt himself choking—only this time with frustration as he realised here was the woman he desired above all others, in his kitchen, raising a glass to salute him and smiling at him.

It was an image he'd begun to see in his dreams, so why wasn't he more pleased by the reality?

'I think it goes, no gain without pain,' he blustered as Rowena sipped at her wine then lowered the glass to the table, leaving her lips sheened with moisture.

'Then I don't believe it,' she said stoutly. 'There are plenty of things you can achieve without the slightest hint of pain. What about kissing?'

David glanced down at the glass to check how much wine she'd actually imbibed.

Very little!

'What about kissing?' he managed to ask, while the inner turmoil in his chest, to say nothing of an aching heaviness in his loins, threatened to overwhelm him.

'There's no pain in kissing,' Rowena told him, lifting the glass again and taking another sip. Only this time she kept her eyes on him, watching, over the rim of the glass, for his reaction to her words. 'But surely there's a gain as far as moving a relationship along.'

'I suppose so,' he agreed reluctantly—extraordinarily disappointed to find she was merely using kissing as an example in her argument.

'So?' she asked, setting the glass down again.

'So?' he echoed, totally lost now.

'So, after all the hints Sarah was dropping, aren't you going to kiss me?' his nurse-receptionist asked, then she smiled encouragingly at him while her eyes twinkled wickedly, probably with delight at his predicament.

'Of course I'm not going to kiss you,' he said crossly, because it was bad enough to be fighting the dictates of his body without having to battle her as well. 'We don't have a relationship. It's just impossible, Rowena, you must see that!'

'Why?'

He closed his eyes and took a very deep breath.

'Why what?'

'Why's it impossible?'

She leaned closer as she asked the question and he could see down the front of her shirt to the deep cleft between her breasts. Desire tightened his body again, while frustration blew the lid off his temper.

'Because there are too many question marks hanging over my head,' he roared. 'I thought I could sort it out—put it behind me. It's why I wanted time off—to finalise things once and for all. To go into the legal ramifications of Sue-Ellen's disappearance—whether divorce is possible, or if I have to have her declared dead, all that kind of thing. I have to move her things—her grandfather's collection—from this property. I wanted to start again, Rowena, as a new man—or as new as a battered being like myself could ever be. Then I could... Perhaps we could...'

As his voice trailed away Rowena felt her heart jerk to a halt, then start beating again with all the verve and crazy rhythm of a tap-dancer. Was he saying he *did* feel something for her? That she *hadn't* judged him wrongly, and made a total idiot of herself by suggesting the kiss?

'So what's different now?' she asked, though she already knew the answer.

'Mary-Ellen's arrival!' David replied. 'That's what's different now. She hasn't come to wish me well in my future, Rowena. She's come to stir up trouble. I always felt she was the gentler of the two of them—the more sympathetic, if anyone brought up as indulgently as they were could be seen as sympathetic. But when Sue-Ellen disappeared, Mary-Ellen turned into an avenging fury, and I realised, familiar though she might have seemed, I hadn't known her at all.'

He paused, and nodded to Sarah who had come back into the big room.

'And unless I miss my guess, her "friend" is a detective, isn't he, Sarah? Did you recognise the species?'

At Sarah's answering nod, David touched Rowena on the arm, wanting physical contact as he made the meaning of his reluctance plain.

'She hasn't brought a detective to help her go through old farm machinery. She accused me of murder once, now she's after proof,'

'Which she won't find!' Rowena said stoutly, but David had been there before and knew just how ugly the smallest incident could be made to look once suspicions were aroused.

'I wouldn't be too sure of that,' he murmured, then he

shrugged his shoulders and added, 'But isn't there another saying about "sufficient unto the day is the evil thereof"? Let's talk about something else or we won't be able to enjoy whatever delicious concoction you've got simmering in that pot.'

Rowena turned away, lifting plates from the warming oven and setting them out on a cooler part of the stove while she served the meal. She'd been through hell when she'd lost Peter and Adrian, so much so the realisation that she might one day fall in love again had come as a shock to her.

At first she'd decided it was simply empathy she felt for David, born of the shared tragedies in their lives. But lately her body had got into the act, becoming heavy with longing when they were apart and unreliably skittish whenever they were together.

Behind her, Sarah had asked a question about a patient, diverting at least part of David's mind from the arrival of trouble in the form of Mary-Ellen.

'What about hepatitis?' Sarah was saying, as Rowena set the plates down in front of the two doctors and turned her mind from fruitless conjecture about her future—about love—to medical matters. 'Has the family been away anywhere?'

'Are you talking about young Mick Alistair?' Rowena asked, and, on Sarah's nod, she added, 'The Alistairs never go away. They settled here to escape the rat race, though what the kids will do when they grow up is anyone's guess.'

'We had another youngster—wasn't it the Williams girl, Rowena? Anyway, she came in recently with similar symptoms of listlessness and general debility. I sent a blood test to the mainland and asked for liver function but it came back negative for any hepatitis.'

'Did you retest? Or perhaps you'd missed the boat. Raised serum levels usually only show in the acute phase, which could have passed before the patient came to see you.'

'What about appearance? Isn't there a jaundiced look in hepatitis sufferers?' Rowena asked, glad they had medicine to discuss.

'End of summer—a lot of people look jaundiced as the summer tan wears off!' David negated that suggestion.

'Great!' Rowena said. 'The yellow look always did suit me.'

'Dark urine and pale faeces are the best indicators,' Sarah offered, and David chuckled.

'Lovely topic for the dinner table,' he said, but Rowena guessed they all preferred it to the one that hovered in their heads.

Sarah diverted the conversation to less medical topics by asking about sightseeing—and walks Lucy and Tony could do with a small boy in a backpack. Then David excused himself, promising to do the dishes the following night and muttering an excuse neither of the women could understand.

'What's the bet he's cleaning out a room for me as far as possible from his?' Rowena said to Sarah.

'More fool he,' Sarah responded, but she looked concerned enough to bother Rowena.

'Have I done the wrong thing?' she asked. 'Coming out like this? Forcing myself on him?'

Sarah smiled at her.

'I don't think so, although you have to see it from his side as well. If he has any feelings at all for you—and he has a fondness, that much is obvious—then he'd want to protect you from whatever it is he fears.'

'Protect me? That's nonsense. What's there to protect me from—apart from a little gossip? Anyway, what woman wants protection these days?'

'All of us at times,' Sarah replied, taking the teatowel from Rowena's hand and waving her away. 'Though it's getting harder for us to admit it. And it's even harder to convince a protective man of the times we *don't* need it. Like now, in your case. If he's off somewhere making up a bed, maybe you should join him—offer to help. Very seductive places, bedrooms.'

Sarah made it sound so easy, but as Rowena left the room she felt far from certain about this idea. First she'd forced her way into his house, now she was going to, well, seduce him, if she could.

If that was the only way she could make him see how she felt about him...

She found him in what was obviously the main bedroom, for it was big enough to have a couple of easy chairs grouped near a wide window which looked out over the dark fields and beyond them to the ever-present, but currently invisible sea.

'I'm clearing my stuff out of here so Sarah can have this room—there's more space for when her family comes and a small room off it for James.'

David had emerged from a walk-in wardrobe with his arms full of clothes, so the explanation was largely unnecessary. Except that he was probably feeling as awkward as she was.

'Let me help,' she suggested, stepping towards him and putting out her hands to take the clothes.

He passed them to her, but their arms became entangled so they were held close, but not too close, in the middle of the spacious room. David's dark eyes scanned her face, slowly and deliberately, as if seeing her for the first time.

Or fixing an image in his mind? Something to keep?

'You have to go,' he said, his voice so husky with emotion it seemed to trail its threads against her skin.

'No,' she whispered, forcing the word through vocal cords tight with desire.

'Please?'

This time she couldn't speak at all, so she shook her head

and moved her hands through the clothing until she could grip his forearms.

'Rowena!'

He breathed her name so softly it was like an echo of a light summer breeze skimming across the sea.

'David,' she murmured back, leaning into the clothes to close the gap between them.

'I can't...' he muttered, the sound strangled by emotion, but Rowena had committed herself to this action so she ignored the denial and took the initiative, pressing closer—close enough to stop any further protests with a kiss.

His response burned against her lips, starting a trembling deep inside her body and a hunger she knew no food would satisfy. Her hands still gripped his arms, and the wedge of clothing remained between them, but his kiss told her things he'd never mentioned—things she'd dared not hope he felt.

It filled her with a joy so wondrous her body felt light enough to float. It sought out the still bruised parts of her heart and eased the last vestiges of pain.

Pain!

Not all the pain.

She broke away.

'Sorry! It was one of the coat-hangers,' she explained apologetically as she lifted the clothes away from him and dumped them on the bed. 'The wretched thing was digging into me in a very vulnerable place.'

She rubbed at the underside of her breast, making a joke of it, but if she'd hoped to see amusement in David's dark eyes she was doomed to disappointment. He was staring at her as if he couldn't remember who she was—his eyes glazed by what she guessed were memories.

Of Sue-Ellen kissing him in this same room?

Rowena turned and gathered up the discarded clothes, silently cursing herself for being all kinds of a fool.

'Where do you want them? Have you cleaned out a room?'

David had watched her move away, dump the clothes, then regather them. Now he heard the words—his neurones were synapsing sufficiently well for his hearing to work—but he couldn't rally enough brain-power to respond.

Not when his body was on fire from a single kiss, while his mind grappled with its implications. One thing was certain—he had to keep his hands off Rowena, at least until Mary-Ellen and her detective friend had left the island.

It was mention of the coat-hanger that had sent his mind spinning out of control, images from the past appearing so vividly that the present seemed pale by comparison.

She'd stood in this room, Mary-Ellen, a small avenging fury with her arms full of her sister's clothes and a single, padded, pale lilac coat-hanger held like a baton in her right hand.

'You'll never get over this!' she'd told him, waving the coat-hanger to emphasise her words. 'Never, never, never!'

Then, as he'd backed away from the lilac weapon, she'd stepped closer and poked the tip of the coat-hanger under his chin—a very vulnerable place.

'Because I will never, never let you!'

And in that instant he'd realised she was as unstable as her sister had been. That Mary-Ellen, the twin he'd thought the rational one, was probably as crazy as his wife.

He blinked away the memory and rubbed his hands across his face, dry-washing it as if to remove something unsavoury.

Rowena had to go. Sarah had seen something in his behaviour to make her suspect his interest in his colleague, and he couldn't risk Mary-Ellen guessing, or even suspecting, how he felt. For Mary-Ellen hadn't made her threat lightly, and to expose his feelings for Rowena was to expose her to risk.

The thought started a clangour of fear along his nerves, while an icy coldness swept through his veins.

He followed her out of the room and across the hall to where he'd earlier flung open the windows on a musty, long-closed room and stripped the covers off the bed, preparatory to making it.

'I've hung your things in the wardrobe. How about you shift the rest of your clothes while I make the bed?' Rowena suggested, not even turning to look at him. 'Sarah found the linen cupboard and she's making up a bed for me in the small bedroom further down the hall. Actually, she was making it up for herself until I told her you were shifting out of yours, so—'

'You can't stay,' he said harshly, cutting through the rush of explanation—aware he'd said the words before and been ignored.

'Are you going to physically toss me out?' she demanded, turning to face him.

He shrugged.

'You know I wouldn't do that.'

'Good!' A decisive nod, more like the Rowena he knew from work—the practical and sensible Rowena, not the one with kisses like liquid fire—accompanied the word. 'Because I'm not going.'

Desperate times called for desperate measures! The overworked saying rang in his head, causing him to wonder if stress reduced brain-power to such an extent that clichés were all it could dredge up. He'd certainly come up with a few weak ones this evening!

He'd have to make it obvious to Mary-Ellen there was nothing going on between himself and Rowena—not that there was, apart from one kiss.

And to make it clear to her, it would also have to be very clear to Rowena. He couldn't remember what he'd said earlier—how much of his attraction he'd confessed.

But so what if he contradicted himself now—as long as he could keep her safe.

'Well, if you won't leave the house,' he said, hoping he sounded clinically cool not maniacally irrational, 'would you at least leave my bedroom? I had a sensible mother who believed boys should be able to look after themselves. I've been making my own bed for thirty years.'

Rowena flinched—at the steely cadence of his voice as much as at the words themselves, although they were cruel enough.

She glanced towards him, but one look at the grim set of his face was enough to stifle any protest.

'Please yourself!' she said, as lightly as her churning emotions would allow, then she flung the second sheet down on the bed and walked out of the room, taking care not to brush against him as she went.

It was the kiss that had done it—it had to be. Up till then, he'd been against her staying, and he'd argued angrily, but he'd still been David. Not the cold, imperious stranger who'd *ordered* her out of his bedroom.

His bedroom? Of course!

Oh, how could she have been so dumb? David had been so obviously shocked by the arrival of his missing wife's twin that it *had* to have brought back memories of his marriage. Then, on top of that, she, Rowena Stupid Jackman, had been insensitive enough to kiss him in the bedroom he'd shared, if only for a few short breaks, with the woman he'd loved.

Pain lodged beneath her ribs, and lumped its way into her throat as she walked blindly down the hall that ran through the centre of this bedroom wing.

She heard the growl of a vacuum cleaner coming from one of the rooms further down the hall—the cleanest of the closed-off rooms, according to Sarah.

Hurt, embarrassed and troubled, Rowena hesitated outside the door. She could take over Sarah's job and clean the room herself. Or fling herself into Sarah's arms and weep away at least some of her frustration. Tempting, but hardly mature behaviour, Rowena! And it would also mean having to confess about the kiss to Sarah, and right now she was feeling so embarrassed about forcing the issue that she'd far rather try to blot it from her mind.

She wandered out to the wide veranda encircling the house and gazed out over dark paddocks that seemed eerily quiet and other-worldly beneath a cloud-stacked sky.

Great! Just what she needed—the weather was closing in and Mary-Ellen Whoever-she-was-these-days would probably be stuck on the island for weeks, reminding David on a daily basis of the woman he'd loved.

And somehow lost!

Literally.

CHAPTER THREE

ROWENA rose early, although the dark clouds massing above shut out any glimpse of the sun, and the morning was dark, cold and clammy with the fog, wisping and twirling above the paddocks.

She dressed, then debated whether she should sit in her bedroom until she heard sounds of movement from one of the other two inhabitants of the house or if she could sneak out to the kitchen and make herself a cup of tea.

Sitting on the bed would only exacerbate her already strung-out nerves, so she opted for the sneaking.

'Ha! So I'm not the only one who wakes early,' Sarah greeted her, from her perch beside the warm stove. 'Actually, David's up as well. I heard him banging around outside, presumably feeding or watering his animals. Is his sheep one of the milking kind, do you know?'

'Yes, but he's a ram, not a sheep, remember,' Rowena replied. 'Or he was until David doctored it. In fact, it was a stud sheep, one of a neighbour's herd, but the darned thing was uncontrollable. Always breaking down fences or escaping under them and coming over here to David's place.'

'He was in love with my pig,' David said, coming in on the conversation in time to explain. 'Still is, poor chap! Though the pig won't have a bar of him.'

He spoke lightly but the signs of a sleepless night were clearly visible in the drawn lines of his face and a greyness in his cheeks.

'What time are you two off to work?'

Rowena turned to Sarah.

'You're the boss. I usually get in about half an hour

before the first patient so I can get out the files and tidy up any outstanding paperwork. How about you?'

'Half an hour early—that's about eight.' Sarah glanced at her watch. 'And fifteen minutes' travelling—we'll leave in twenty minutes.'

She was answering David but then turned to Rowena.

'Are you happy to take me? I've a hire car booked but haven't got around to collecting it from the garage. In fact, there was some mix-up with the booking as I'd wanted a four-wheel drive and they only had a small sedan available.'

Nice normal conversation, Rowena thought as she nodded to Sarah and waved the teapot towards David to offer him a cup. Behind her, the toaster popped out an evenly browned piece of toast, and to any alien hovering above, the scene would have been one of earthly normality.

But the air in the room was brittle with tension, so much so she was surprised it didn't crackle when she moved.

Sarah broke it by teasing David about the pig, then asking how he'd come by it.

'A present from a friend who thought a small piglet was the perfect going-away present to someone daft enough to go and live on an island.'

'Didn't this friend realise it would grow?' Sarah asked, and David shrugged his broad shoulders.

'City folk!' he said, using the islanders' explanation for the vagaries of all their visitors.

'And the native animals?' Sarah persisted, apparently determined to keep the conversation going.

'They're only temporary residents. People tend to bring them to me when they're found injured but alive. I either patch them up or, if they're too bad, put them down humanely. Once the injured ones are fit and well, they go back to the bush—or that's the theory. I've a wombat in a log behind the shed who has no intention of ever going bush. I mean, why root around in tough forest country when you can find plenty of food in my lush green paddocks?'

'Well, James will love them all. Speaking of hollow logs, do you have many on the property? I wouldn't mind taking some back to use as planters.'

As Sarah continued to question David, Rowena's thoughts drifted back to the previous night. To the early part of it, when David had said he was tidying up his life for a reason—and almost intimating that the reason was her.

Which must mean he cared...

Though perhaps she'd misunderstood, which would explain his coldness now...

'Coming?'

Sarah's voice suggested she was repeating her question, and Rowena stood up, crossed hastily to the sink, washed her cup and plate, then, muttering about teeth, hurried from the room.

This was no time for dreams—not when the reality was that David didn't want her here.

Though, for his sake, and his future on the island, she was staying, whether he liked it or not.

'You OK?'

Sarah's question dragged David out of gloomy introspection—brought on by the sight of Rowena's shapely figure exiting through the kitchen door.

'No!' he said, because he was so far from OK a lie would have been obvious. 'But, hopefully, I'll get there eventually.'

He read the concern in Sarah's eyes, and tried what he hoped would prove a reassuring smile.

'Mary-Ellen's arrival threw me, but I'd intended cleaning out the shed—facing up to all the stuff packed away in there—so nothing's really changed except she'll be watching every move I make, and needling me as much as possible.'

'Why?'

Natural question, bluntly delivered.

Why?

'I guess because she honestly believes I killed her sister. I suppose if the same thing had happened to someone I cared about, I'd want it finalised.'

Even as he said the words he realised how terrible they must sound to Sarah. 'I mean, if I thought someone had killed Sue-Ellen, if I suspected someone in particular, I'd want to see justice done.'

'But you don't think she was deliberately killed?'

David sighed and ran his hands through his hair, kneading at his scalp with frustration.

'No! I just can't believe it. There'd be no reason, you see. At first, I thought she'd simply left me—in fact, I suspected that if she had, Mary-Ellen had probably helped her. They came over to the island together—a few days before I was due to fly in. They brought a couple of horses for Sue and I to ride during the holidays, then Mary-Ellen went back with the empty horse float. It would have been easy enough for Sue-Ellen to hide in the float for the trip back on the ferry, even though the ferry crew reckon they'd have seen her because one of the deckhands backed the float on while the other gave directions.'

'Were you having trouble in your marriage that made her leaving you a possibility?'

David gave her a weak smile.

'We were always having trouble,' he admitted. 'From the honeymoon at Aspen onward. I fell in love with a beautiful woman, Sarah, madly in love, and married her without ever knowing her. We were as unalike as two people ever could be, and on top of that she was—'

He stopped short, loyalty to his absent wife preventing him from voicing his professional opinion about her mental state or his personal opinion of her spending habits and her casual attitude towards extramarital affairs!

Sarah didn't press him.

'You say at first you believed she'd simply left you. What changed your mind?'

He thought back.

'Mary-Ellen's behaviour, I suppose. She was hysterical, hurling accusations, acting nearly demented with grief. At first I thought it was all show—put on to convince me she didn't know anything. But I felt a tension behind it all—it's hard to explain, especially as both of them could throw tantrums. But this was different—it made me believe Mary-Ellen's behaviour was genuine—and I couldn't believe Sue-Ellen would go off and not contact her sister at some stage.'

'To let her know she was all right? They were close?'

David let his gaze drift around the room, remembering the scenes played out whenever the pair had been together.

'There was a bond—an almost unbreakable link—so even when they fought and at times acted as if they hated each other, it held them together. I used to think Sue-Ellen was jealous of her sister—Mary-Ellen was married to a prince or duke or whatever at the time. When Mary-Ellen phoned to say she was leaving him and coming home, Sue was delighted, but I had a feeling the delight was partly because her sister's marriage had failed.'

'Complex things, twins!' Sarah said, and David gave a huff of laughter.

'Tell me about it! But the other thing that bothered me about her disappearance was that she'd done it from the island. Because, apart from private yachts sneaking in at midnight and even then a fishing boat would probably have seen it, people's comings and goings are monitored by flight or ferry tickets. If you were going to disappear, it would be far easier to do it from the mainland—hire a car in a false name, drive to another town and fly somewhere.'

Sarah nodded slowly.

'So because she disappeared from here, it was more likely she'd died?'

'The island's a hazardous place,' he explained. 'She could have been walking along one of the cliff paths and slipped into the sea. Injured herself in a fall in the bush and not been able to get to help. These were the things that tormented me, Sarah, but I couldn't get anyone to listen. Especially as Mary-Ellen pooh-poohed the idea her sister would walk anywhere!'

He let his breath out in a long, regretful sigh.

'Oh, they searched, but I felt it was perfunctory. To the authorities, once they took her disappearance seriously, there was only one feasible answer. Especially when the city police found a man who confessed to being her lover and who claimed she was going to leave me for him.'

He drew a deep ragged breath.

'They assumed I'd murdered her and hidden her body so, instead of looking at places where she might be found alive, they dug up any recently turned-over ground, and searched the farm, the bottom of the wells and any handy ravines for her body.'

'It must have been hell for you,' Sarah said, reaching out to touch his hand.

'I'm ready!'

Rowena reappeared, and the pain of loss stabbed into David's ribs. But he had to do it, had to stay aloof from her no matter how hard it was—or what level of pain he detected in her eyes. He was diverted from these bitter thoughts by the sound of a vehicle approaching up the long drive leading to the house.

'We'll get going,' Sarah said quickly. 'Come on, Rowena. Let's leave him to his fate.'

'That's not a very nice expression!' David protested, but if he'd had his way they'd have been gone long before Mary-Ellen arrived. He just hadn't expected her this early on such a gloomy, overcast day.

And thank heavens Sarah hadn't asked about the weather.

'Help! Where did this wind come from?' Sarah demanded, as she clutched her coat around her body and struggled across the yard towards the car.

'Blew up an hour ago—you'll notice the mist's gone,' Rowena responded. 'Though this is only a breeze compared to what is probably on the way.'

'A breeze? Don't ever let me out in a gale!' Sarah yelled, grabbing the car door as the wind tried to snatch it out of her hands.

They sat in the car and waited until the mud-splashed Range Rover reached the end of the drive and pulled up at the bottom of the shallow front steps.

'It's only plebs like us who use the tradesmen's entrance round the back,' Rowena muttered, starting the engine and taking off as if anxious to leave the house and its visitors far behind her.

'David will manage her better today,' Sarah said, giving Rowena's knee a comforting pat. 'He was shaken yesterday, thinking it was his wife when he'd thought she was dead for all these years.'

'Why?'

The puzzled look Sarah shot her told Rowena she'd been too blunt, but it was a question which had niggled in her head all night.

'I mean, why would he presume she was dead, not just missing?'

'He was just explaining it to me. I think it's mainly because she didn't contact her sister—didn't contact anyone, of course, but most particularly her sister. They were too close for her to go on living and not let her sister know. Well, I think that's what David thinks and I assume that's what the police believed or they wouldn't have gone through with a murder investigation.'

'They did it because of Mary-Ellen's demands!' Rowena

said bitterly. 'The family had connections everywhere—and money to burn—so, of course, the police and politicians all listened to her rather than to David.'

'Do you remember it? The investigations here on the island?'

Rowena thought back.

'I guess I do, but my main memories are of sympathy for David. It was only twelve months after Peter and Adrian went missing—I was still hurting and it brought it all back. For Peter, the locals who have planes did air searches and the fishermen scoured the coastline, but with Sue-Ellen there were squads of imported folk stumbling around the countryside, looking for a grave, as I remember, while helicopters buzzed overhead and boats searched the sea for a body.'

They drove into the little township as she finished her explanation, and pulled up behind the surgery.

'But enough of that—of the bad memories. Let's think about today. Mrs Alistair's bringing Mick back in—the child with suspected hepatitis. He's the first patient. If the blood test's negative, will you retest or not?'

'I don't think it's worth it,' Sarah told her when they'd dashed from the car to the building, against a wind that now included big splattering drops of rain. 'It's more than likely the acute phase has passed and we've missed that kind of diagnosis. Also, as there's little we can do to treat it, except advise rest and plenty of fluids, there's no point. Didn't David say something about another child?'

'The Williams girl,' Rowena confirmed as she unlocked the door and led them inside. 'But why not treatment? There are treatments for hep. B and some of the other forms of the disease. Can we be sure it's not something treatable?'

Sarah nodded, understanding what Rowena was thinking—understanding also that they were talking about a little boy not much older than her son had been when he'd been lost at sea.

'Other forms would have shown up in the blood. I'll certainly double-check the test results, but if this is the second case, I should also have a look around at common denominators to see if we can find a carrier.'

She took the file Rowena handed her and flipped it open.

'A carrier? You mean someone else who's affected?' Rowena asked.

'Someone who has it, perhaps as part of a general infection. Has there been an outbreak of rubella recently, or is there someone you know of with Epstein-Barr virus?'

'Epstein-Barr—heavens! I haven't heard of that for years. Mostly the islanders get common things like colds and flu, the occasional broken arm or leg and, of course, have farm and fishing boat accidents.'

'Actually, Epstein-Barr's most common early form is glandular fever—and it's from the same viral family as cold sores.'

They were back at work, Rowena realised as she listened to Sarah's explanations. And for the next eight hours, because the islanders were curious about the new locum and would pop in on the slightest of pretexts, she should be too busy to think about David Wright—or the romance that had ended before it had even begun.

Apart from one kiss!

The arrival of a third tired and listless child suggested the hepatitis was originating at the school all three attended.

'Maybe the carrier is someone handling food up there,' Sarah told Rowena as they ate their own lunch in the little café up the road. 'Do they have a tuckshop?'

Rowena nodded.

'But Bessie Jenkins who runs it is the cleanest of souls.'

Sarah smiled.

'I'm not accusing Bessie of being dirty, but perhaps when we finish here you could go up and have a talk to her. Find out if she's wearing gloves while she prepares sandwiches and serves food. If it's not a food handler, it could be a contaminated water supply, which would involve official notice to the health authorities.'

'But you've patients all afternoon,' Rowena protested.

'No worries! If you leave the stack of files, I can see them in. It's not as if there's anything in the waiting room anyone would want to pinch. I leafed through a magazine yesterday then realised it was years out of date when I saw an article on Princess Di.'

Returning to the surgery, Sarah worked through another hour of patients with wounds, aches and pains she suspected would have been ignored were it not for her novelty value. Her arrival hadn't been announced so the two days she'd spent with David had been her only introduction. Word had now spread and islanders, who had as much curiosity as anyone, were coming to check on her.

'Just rest it,' she was telling Mrs Armstrong, who was complaining of pain 'moving up and down my arm', when she heard the bell ring on the outer door as it was opened.

Assuming it was Rowena returning, or another patient, she was surprised, when she ushered Mrs Armstrong out, to see David slumped on a stool in the small storeroom. His head was bowed, his shoulders hunched and he radiated pain so palpable Sarah caught her breath.

'I'll be out for the next patient in a minute,' she said, poking her head into the waiting room where an elderly couple sat, hand in hand.

Then she went into the storeroom, put her arm around David and urged him off the stool.

'You can't sit there. Come in and tell me what's wrong. You can go out again through the back door so you don't have to see anyone.'

'I can't go out again,' he said, allowing her to lead him into his own consulting room. 'You have to go. Out to the farm. They need you there. I'm sorry, Sarah!'

The words were as dry as desert dust, flat and toneless—not making sense.

He staggered forward with the gait of a hundred-year-old and slumped again—this time into his chair.

'I'll take the rest of the patients.'

He tossed a bunch of keys to her.

'Take my car. Rowena can run me home. If I haven't been arrested.'

Arrested?

Sarah stepped towards him and seized his shoulder to give him a slight shake.

'You're in shock. I can see that, but you've got to snap out of it, David. You can't possibly see patients in this state. There's no one urgent—I can send them home, close the surgery.'

He raised his head and turned pain-filled eyes to hers.

'I need to work,' he told her. 'Need to do something, don't you see?'

Sarah rested her hand against his cheek.

'Tell me,' she said gently. 'Tell me why?'

He shook his head like a bewildered animal, then breathed deeply. As she watched he almost visibly pulled himself together, consciously tightening all the sinew and muscle in his body.

'They've found her,' he said, his voice stronger, level, but still as remote as the Arctic. 'Found Sue-Ellen. Obviously, as chief suspect in what is most probably a murder, I can't help with the forensic side of it. Barry Ryan, our local police sergeant, wants you to take a look.'

'Murder?' Sarah murmured.

'Very few people commit suicide by shutting themselves into a trunk, Sarah!'

A coldness, harsher than the rain beyond the window, seeped into Sarah's body. She searched for words but knew there weren't any to help her friend.

'Are you sure you want to see patients?' she asked him, and he nodded.

She heard the bell again and prayed it was Rowena.

'OK, but first you'll have a hot drink. It won't hurt anyone to wait.'

She left him behind the desk, staring blindly at the few remaining patient files. Rowena was chatting to the elderly couple, still hand in hand, and Sarah had to excuse herself and ask Rowena if she could spare a minute.

She led the surprised nurse out to the kitchen alcove just inside the rear door, and filled her in on what had happened.

Rowena's reaction mirrored David's, although Sarah knew Rowena's pain was for her boss, not for herself or the dead woman.

'Take him in a cup of coffee and see if you can get him to eat something—a couple of sweet biscuits. It will help with the shock. And keep an eye on him. Send the patients home if necessary, or rebook them for this evening. I can come back and see anyone urgent then.'

Rowena seemed to understand so Sarah left, assuming that activity of some kind out at David's place would show her where to go when she got there.

The activity—in the form of the Range Rover they'd seen earlier, an ambulance and one of the big four-wheel-drive police vehicles parked by the bigger of the two sheds behind David's house—suggested Sue-Ellen's body had been found there.

In a trunk, David had said.

An old-fashioned cabin trunk, perhaps.

What would a cabin trunk be doing in what Sarah had assumed was a machinery shed?

She parked beside the police vehicle and walked towards the open doors.

'Because it's where someone, perhaps the twins' grandfather, kept all his junk.' She answered her own question as she viewed the contents of the shed for the first time.

There were crates and cartons, old machinery of every description, buggies and drays once drawn by horses, and yokes obviously made for oxen.

And that was just at first glance.

What looked like an old stagecoach took up most of one corner, but the majority of the paraphernalia was smaller and stacked in teetering towers. An ancient perambulator topped a chest which was set on a table while underneath crouched a piece of metal which might have come direct from the torture chambers of the Spanish Inquisition, though Sarah assumed it could just as easily be a farm implement of some kind.

The smell reached her nostrils at the same time as a voice registered in her ears.

'Dr Kemp?'

The policeman, whom she'd seen in town but not met, appeared from behind a drum on wheels—a mobile silo? He was followed by the ambulance attendant, who nodded a greeting at her and continued on his way—obviously not needed.

'Barry Ryan,' the man in khaki added, holding out his hand, then, realising it was gloved, withdrawing it to nod awkwardly at her.

'It's Sarah,' she said, acknowledging his introduction with a smile and an offer to use her first name. 'David tells me you've got a body.'

'What's left of it,' the man muttered, leading her into the shed and along a narrow corridor left as a walkway through the collection. A harsh rhythmic sound like asthmatic breathing made her look around.

The woman Sarah had glimpsed in the waiting room the previous day was crouched in an old chair at the far end of this particular walkway, the tall man by her side so erect he gave Sarah the impression he was standing guard. The noise was the woman breathing and instinct took Sarah to the living patient first.

'Are you all right? Are you an asthmatic? Have you medication with you?'

The woman looked at her, her dark eyes blank.

Sarah tried the man.

'Do you want to take her over to the house? Fix her a warm drink?'

'I doubt the sergeant wants us in the house,' the man said.

'Oh, for heaven's sake!' Sarah snorted. 'David Wright's been living in the house for the last three years—and I'm not the only visitor he's had in that time. Don't you think any evidence there might have been has disappeared or been destroyed by this time?'

'Destroyed by him!' the woman said bitterly, but her breathing had improved, lessening Sarah's concern.

'You're right, of course.' Barry Ryan had followed Sarah towards the pair and hovered behind her, but he now stepped forward. 'Though I'd prefer it you didn't go into the house, Mr...'

He consulted his notebook then added, 'Page. It might be best if you took...' Another pause while he checked his notes again, then, either because he couldn't read his own writing or couldn't pronounce Mary-Ellen's surname, he opted for the easy way out. 'The lady back to town.'

'We're staying right here,' Mary-Ellen decreed. 'That's my sister there. And finding her like this just proves there was a cover-up the first time the police supposedly searched the place. If you think I'm going to let you get away with it again...'

The threat might have been implied but it was no less real, and Sarah, glancing towards the woman once again, saw sparks, like tiny flares on a dark night, had brought the dull eyes back to life.

'We'll treat her right and not make any mistakes,' Barry promised, but Mary-Ellen showed no sign of moving and he didn't push her.

Instead, he led Sarah back along the walkway, then a couple of steps down another aisle diverging off the first.

'The lady says it's her sister, she recognises the clothes,'

Barry told Sarah. 'David seemed less certain—he's worried about the hair because, he said, his wife was a redhead at the time of the disappearance and the deceased is definitely blonde.'

The policeman was speaking in what he probably thought was an undertone, but for a man used to shouting against the winds which regularly ravaged the island, his undertone had all the boom and carrying power of a megaphone.

'I told you about that!' the woman yelled from her invisible perch beside the wall. 'I told you she met me at the airport when I got back from Austria and the first thing we did was go to a beauty salon and have our hair cut and coloured the same. We always did it when we were together. It was fun!'

Because it fooled people and probably upset them, Sarah thought, remembering what Rowena had said about the twins when they'd been young.

But it wasn't her place to agree or disagree. She ignored the remark, concentrating her attention on Barry.

'What do you want me to do?'

He scratched his head, and shrugged his shoulders as if in discomfort.

'Have a look at it where it is, then maybe again at the hospital. We don't have a proper mortuary, but there's a kind of sluice room out the back with a stainless-steel table, hoses and everything else you'll need. Eventually, the deceased will have to go to the mainland, and we'll get homicide detectives taking over here. I've already phoned the mainland, but a four-year-old body doesn't excite them to the point of chartering a plane to send experts over today. They said for me to do the preliminaries and they'll fly someone over on the scheduled flight tomorrow, though, with the weather closing in, the airport's likely to be closed…'

Sarah listened to the wailing of the wind above the building and knew exactly what he meant. Forget the homicide people not arriving, her family might not make it!

Dismissing the selfish thought, she considered the situation from the policeman's point of view. If planes were unable to land, they were on their own in the investigation until the faithful ferry, *Trusty*, came in next week.

If it was able to come in...

'I need to know it's all there—the whole body,' Barry explained. 'Or if we have to search for more of it. It's not a big trunk, you know.'

'Bodies can fold up pretty small,' Sarah told him, then, knowing she couldn't put it off any longer, she walked across to have a look.

The trunk was small, but the pitiful remains of the once beautiful woman didn't overfill it. Sarah closed her eyes against the sadness that never failed to overwhelm her at the sight of any death, then took a deep breath, knelt and looked more closely at the body.

It was held together by the clothes as much as anything else, but they were disintegrating, contaminated by the destruction of rotting body fluids and an insect infestation which proved the trunk couldn't have been airtight.

Sarah suspected the clothes would fall apart when touched. Scraps of skin and flesh, dried to the consistency of leather, clung here and there to the bones, and the body seemed to curl around itself in a parody of the foetal position, except that the head was turned upwards.

The small face, so perfect in life but now stripped back to desiccated bone, looked back at her. The vivid blonde hair, still falsely bright and pulled forward towards the victim's right eye, made a caricature of the skull.

Using a pen she had in her pocket, Sarah lifted the hair and saw the perfectly round hole just above the temple.

She heard Barry swear but he had the good sense not to comment. But suddenly the need for privacy, the need to do whatever she could for this slain woman, became paramount in Sarah's mind.

'You've taken photos?' she asked the policeman, who nodded towards his constable. Sarah registered the young man for the first time, and saw he was holding Polaroid and video cameras.

'Though if you hold her hair like you did, we'll take a shot of that,' he said, waving the constable forward.

Sarah repeated her movement, while her eyes scanned what she could see of the rest of the body.

'Are you finished with the chest? Have you drawn it in place, marked what's around it? Done your plans?'

She knew the danger of moving anything from a crime scene before the area had been carefully documented, though she had no idea how anyone could 'document' an area like this.

'I've got my sketches,' Barry assured her. 'Me and the lad did the measurements, but I'll have another look around when we've shifted her.'

'What about fingerprints?'

The policeman gave a bark of laughter.

'Look at all this stuff. Who knows when people have wandered in and out of here? And David, the lady and her gentleman friend have all admitted touching the trunk several times this morning. Apparently, David had decided to go through all the stuff, and the lady came to see he didn't throw away anything valuable.'

'They started at one end of this main walkway, David writing everything down and putting a mark against what the lady wanted.'

Sarah wondered about the continued references to 'the lady'. Could Barry not remember her name or was he disinclined to use it?

'Then the lady saw the trunk. It was under other things, some kind of hatstand and a corner cabinet—they're over there.'

He nodded to where the discarded items lay.

'She wanted to look in it so the other gentleman moved the stuff off the top and David went to lift the trunk to bring it out into the walkway where it was easier to open. It was too heavy so the other chap helped, then the lady opened it—so you've three sets of recent prints on it.'

'But there could be older ones as well,' Sarah said cautiously.

'Too right,' Barry agreed. 'Which is why I'm not touching it. Next thing it goes to town and some anorak at the crime lab curses me for my stupidity because I've destroyed his chances of using something special on the surface.'

Sarah understood. Even with her limited knowledge of the techniques of lifting fingerprints, she knew different chemicals had to be used in a specific order as the use of a particular chemical too early could destroy the opportunity to use another more effective one later.

'With new light sources and the latest ways of making fingerprints obvious, I wonder if they'll be able to work out what's recent and what's ancient. Although if the trunk belonged to Mary-Ellen's family, and has been shifted around in here, it's logical that family fingerprints could be on it for innocent reasons.'

'The lady's already explained!' Barry said gloomily. 'Said it was her mother's trunk and they used to keep old clothes in it for her and her sister to dress up. It's why she wanted it out, she said.'

Sarah looked at the trunk and shook her head. It didn't look like a trunk a woman would keep in the house. Particularly not a woman as wealthy as the twins' mother had been.

'Well, if you're all done here, let's take her into town,' Sarah suggested. 'Exactly as she is in the trunk. I'll lift her out onto a sheet of plastic first so no trace evidence is lost. Even the dust around her will have to go to the city crime lab for testing.'

'I'll just see off the others first,' Barry told her, and he walked towards the far end of the corridor where Mary-Ellen and her protector had moved so they could watch what was happening.

The tall man argued and, although Sarah couldn't hear the words, she could read anger in his stance. Barry's voice rumbled back to her, explaining crime scenes to a man who'd probably walked a few in his time.

'You can't stay here and I don't want you in the house either,' Barry said. 'So don't make things difficult for me, mate!'

More conversation, then the couple moved away, Barry following them and remaining in the doorway until Sarah heard an engine come to life, followed by the growl of the departing vehicle.

Yet even with the onlookers gone, Sarah felt edgy and uncomfortable. By rights, the body should go, still in the trunk, straight to the city, but if it wasn't complete the police would have to mount a search for the rest of it—as soon as possible. Now the discovery had been made, the perpetrator would lose the sense of security he'd had for the last four years.

He—or possibly she, Sarah told herself firmly—might panic and change the hiding place of any further evidence. Even destroy evidence by burning the shed.

She wondered for a moment why he—or she—hadn't done exactly that earlier.

And was she mentally substituting the word 'perpetrator' for 'murderer' because she might be describing David?

She looked down at the pathetic collection of bones and asked herself how well she knew David.

As well as anyone knew another human being, she'd have said yesterday. He'd been a student with her—best friend of her first lover, Lucy's father. David had been her strength when Lucy's father had been killed. He'd shared her grief, stood by her through her lonely pregnancy, gladly accepted a role as godfather to Lucy, and over the years had kept in touch, by phone, letter and, these days, email.

For him to shoot someone was unthinkable, but to then fold the slight, lifeless body of a woman he had loved into a trunk? Sarah's head couldn't get around the concept—though, in truth, she had difficulty imagining anyone doing such a thing.

The two policemen, suitably gloved, were lifting the trunk—fairly effortlessly, considering what it contained. She studied it more closely as they moved towards their vehicle and realised that though she'd still been thinking trunk and assuming it to be one of the heavy, old-fashioned steamer trunks, it was, in fact, a more modern container, like a metal toolbox.

She looked back at the packed earth on the floor of the shed, not to where the trunk had been when she'd come in but further into the pyramids of junk. A dark rectangle showed the trunk's original position before David and 'the man'—Paul—had lifted it clear. If scene of crime officers were here, they'd vacuum up the dirt so the lab could have a look at it. Should she take it on herself to suggest it to Barry?

Before she could decide he returned, holding the small vacuum cleaner used for this purpose.

'Just in case,' he said. 'If I don't someone will ask for it. Funny lot, those lab fellows. I've seen some'd go silly over a few grains of dirt.'

He vacuumed efficiently around the outer edges of the original rectangle, then removed one paper bag, sealed it and labelled it carefully to show where the contents had been gathered, and replaced it with a second one. Taking even more care, he now swept the little machine back and forth across the place where the trunk had been.

A third bag collected the dirt from where the trunk had rested temporarily.

'What next?' he said to Sarah, squatting back on his

heels and looking around the crammed shed. 'Anything else we should do right now?'

Sarah also allowed her gaze to roam. She began to hope the body was complete. There were so many hiding places in here, it could take a month to search for missing bones.

'Keep people away?' she said. 'Can you do it successfully, given you're a two-man force and you probably have other work to do? For a start, you should watch me as I take the body out. I don't think that's a job for the young fellow.'

'I can grab some volunteers to keep an eye on the place, though if the vic's been missing for four years, I don't know what a search now is going to yield.'

Sarah looked around again, mentally translating the slang word for 'victim'. Vics and perps—the perpetrator—were linked inextricably in the police vocabulary.

'A murder weapon?' she suggested, thinking aloud. 'Though surely it would have been disposed of long ago. And the place must have been gone over thoroughly four years ago. Mrs Wright disappeared on the island, so wouldn't the search for her have begun right here?'

Barry shook his head.

'Before my time, I'm afraid, though the records of what took place will be in the office. But, yes, you're right, after the house and yard, they'd have had to go through all this stuff. Including, you'd think, any trunks and boxes.'

His look told Sarah he didn't relish repeating the exercise, but she was thinking of something else—of a woman going missing.

'How hard would they have searched? Do the police take missing persons' reports of adults all that seriously?'

Barry shrugged.

'It's not something they spend a lot of time on, not in the city. People leave their partners all the time, teenage kids run away. The police put out a bulletin advising the person's gone, but active searches?'

He shook his head.

'Not for adults—not straight away.'

'But here it must have been different, surely?' Sarah persisted. 'After all, she came to the island—everyone knew that—but she didn't leave.'

Barry nodded this time, a very small nod, and Sarah didn't know him well enough to read the nuances of his body language.

'They'd have searched. In fact, I remember enough about it to know they did. Anyway, someone goes missing on the island, you've got to look. Might be lying injured somewhere.'

He frowned, looking down at the mark in the dirt where the trunk had been lying.

'But they didn't find her, did they?' he said. 'Not then, they didn't.'

He picked up his evidence bags, tucked the little vacuum cleaner under his arm and strode towards the door.

CHAPTER FOUR

ROWENA carried the coffee and biscuits into David's consulting room. He was sitting at the desk, elbows on the pile of files, head resting on his hands.

'Here, drink this,' she said brusquely. 'I can cancel the afternoon patients. I don't think you're fit to see anyone.'

He lifted his head and looked at her, as if trying to place where the noise was coming from, then his eyelids drifted down over his eyes and he dropped his head to his hands again.

The pain she'd seen in that telling moment made Rowena wince.

The agonising depth of it made her wonder if he would ever get over the death of his wife—ever recover enough to love again!

Though she'd once thought *she* wouldn't...

'Thanks for the coffee,' he said at last, raising his head again, only this time looking past her towards the door. 'A hot drink—panacea for most ills. Give me five minutes to drink it, then show the Carters in. I'd better see as many people as possible before word gets around. They sure as hell won't want to see me afterwards, and Sarah could be caught up with the police.'

His voice was harsh, like talons scraping across wood. Much as Rowena longed to offer words of comfort or support, she couldn't think of any to fit the situation. She nodded and walked away, so heart-sore she was surprised to find she could still function normally—to all outward appearances anyway.

'David will only be a few minutes longer,' she told the

Carters. 'He's taking over for the afternoon as his locum was called away.'

'Someone sick somewhere, was there?' Mrs Carter asked.

It was a predictable question. With only one doctor on the island, the patients were used to having to wait, or even come back later, when David was called to an emergency. But now Rowena found herself unable to answer. Even nodding would be tantamount to a lie, and as the news would undoubtedly spread like wildfire, the couple would soon know it for what it was.

Rejecting total honesty as an option—unsure what story might spread—she simply smiled at the elderly pair and said, 'I'm afraid I can't talk about it—though, no doubt, everyone will know soon enough.'

Wrong move! she realised as they immediately began speculating, casting sidelong glances in her direction with each guess to see if they could catch a reaction. It was obvious from some of the comments that they knew Mary-Ellen was back on Three Ships and inevitably tied her into things.

'Though,' Mrs Carter said, 'if it was to do with her and her sister, it would be David gone, not the new lady.'

'Stop right now!' Rowena told them. 'Heavens! Gossip in this place must fly through the air. With two thousand people and seven hundred households, I'm sure it couldn't be communicated so quickly by word of mouth.'

The pleased look on Mrs Carter's face told Rowena she'd made a mistake, interrupting at that stage, but behind her she heard the consulting room door open and knew David was ready.

'Go on in,' she said, biting back an urge to warn them not to ask questions—to beg them to be nice to him.

However, knowing it would only provoke more speculation, she held her tongue, closed the door behind them and turned to greet the next patient, who'd come in, late, with Bessie Jenkins from the school tuckshop.

'Thought if you wanted to do your vampire thing on me I might as well get it over and done with straight away,' Bessie said, while Margo Ryan, the policeman's wife and heavily pregnant with her first child, waddled to a chair and settled into it.

'Sorry I'm late but I was asleep,' Margo explained. 'My back's been aching and I couldn't get comfortable last night.'

Rowena looked at the young woman and wondered if she'd have the same difficulties this coming night, though for different reasons.

After offering Margo a drink of water, which was refused, Rowena took Bessie into the treatment room where she took two vials of blood. If the plane came in the following day, they would be sent away to test for hepatitis—if not, they would have to wait. Although David could and did do his own simple blood tests here on the island. Would Sarah continue the practice during her tenure?

Rowena chatted to Bessie as she worked, although her heart wasn't in the conversation. Too busy worrying about David, and how he was handling the Carters' curiosity.

'Whatever the tests show, would you mind asking all the parents who help at the tuckshop to wear gloves all the time they're handling food? And make sure there's someone appointed to handle the money and nothing else. Let the kids queue up to pay at the cash register like you do in a cafeteria.'

'But it takes far longer than having whoever serves them handling the money,' Bessie pointed out. 'And we all know enough to take a glove off for the money.'

'Maybe your helpers don't all follow the rules,' Rowena suggested, though she suspected it might be Bessie herself, used to the way she'd always done things, who occasionally 'forgot' the gloves.

'Are you going to test all the helpers?' the older woman demanded, when Rowena failed to agree and reassure her.

'I only take the blood,' she said, using delegation of responsibility as an excuse. 'It's up to the doctors to decide who to test.'

'Hmmph!' Bessie muttered, although she obediently held the cotton ball over the needle puncture, then held out her arm for Rowena to tape the dressing in place.

They were just leaving the treatment room when Margo gave a loud cry and slid into an uncomfortable crouch on the floor.

The Carters, who had timed their departure to perfection, reached her first, Mrs Carter bending down as if to help Margo to her feet.

'I'll leave you to it,' Bessie said, hurrying out so the ringing of the bell punctuated Margo's distress.

'Let her be for a minute,' Rowena warned the older couple, crossing the room and kneeling on the opposite side of the young woman.

'Was it a strong pain or just unexpected?' she asked when the sheen on Margo's upper lip confirmed it had been a pain-generated cry.

'Oh, it hurt!' Margo moaned.

'Has it gone now?' Rowena asked, glancing up in time to see David take in the scene then cross to the phone.

'Yes, but I don't want to move in case it hurts again,' the young woman said.

Rowena hid a sigh. With some women, all the childbirth lectures and exercises in the world wouldn't prepare them for the pain and discomfort of giving birth.

'OK, let's have a look,' David said, crossing the room with his long, confident stride.

'I'll just get you to sign a Medicare form,' Rowena said to Mr Carter. 'If you could both come over here.'

She led the interested onlookers away, though her thoughts were with the man who now squatted beside

Margo, murmuring soothingly to her, assuring her she'd be all right.

'I've phoned Nell and left a message on her answering machine to let her know you've started labour,' he told her, mentioning the midwife who had delivered the island's babies for the last three decades. 'But this pain is probably only an early warning, so how about I help you up, then have a look at you? Once we know what's happening, you can decide whether you want to go home and wait for a while or go straight to the hospital.'

'I want Barry,' Margo said tearfully. She was standing now, clutching David's arm as if he were the only thing keeping her afloat in a sea of confusion.

'We'll let him know what's happening and I'm sure he'll be here as soon as possible.'

'Do you know where he is?' Mrs Carter asked, far too eagerly. 'We could go and tell him.'

She stepped towards Margo as if to shake the truth out of her.

'He went out to—' Margo began, but Rowena stepped between them.

'I think it's best if we tell him,' she said to the Carters. 'If he's not within mobile range, we can get him on the two-way. Now, Mrs Carter, do you want me to put you down for another appointment? Did David say he wants to see you again?'

She hustled the inquisitive pair away, and was relieved when David helped Margo to her feet and led her towards the consulting room.

'We have to come again next week,' Mrs Carter said. 'I do hope the lady doctor's back here by then.'

'I'm sure she will be,' Rowena assured her.

She waited until they'd departed, then followed David into the consulting room.

Margo was sitting on the examination table, and though

her eyes were now relatively free of tears, Rowena guessed it wouldn't be long before she was crying again.

'I think I'll go to the hospital,' Margo told David. 'I'll feel better there. Safer.'

'Well, just bear in mind you won't be in true labour for many hours yet and you might get bored at the hospital,' David said. His face was pale, and his voice tight with tension, but the hand he rested on Margo's shoulder was gently comforting.

The patient's eyes brimmed again, and he added, 'But if it's what you want to do.'

He turned towards Rowena and she felt actual pain when she read the depths of the despair in his usually gentle brown eyes. His life was in turmoil but his compassion for his patients remained. She wanted to hold him, to warm him with her body and protect him with her arms, but she had no rights as far as he was concerned.

None but her love, which he'd already rejected.

'Are you busy or could you go back to Margo's place with her while she gets her things?' he asked, and Rowena realised he was acting far more professionally than she was, although he'd had by far the greater shock.

She switched her mind back to 'nurse' mode.

'No problem. There are three more patients due, but you can let them in yourself.' She moved forward, but the switch hadn't worked properly because she couldn't resist an urge to touch him, to rest her hand briefly on his forearm.

'You'll know where I am,' she told him, hoping he'd remember the words she'd spoken the previous afternoon when she'd promised to do whatever she could. Hoping he'd realise they still applied.

She felt his muscles tense beneath her fingers, and the air between them seemed to hum with tension. Then David moved his arm away—a slight shift in body angle, nothing more—and she took the hint, hid her hurt and turned to their patient.

'Come on, Margo. Have you got your hospital bag packed? Were you ready for this?'

Margo immediately launched into a long explanation which began with the information that her mother had always gone over her due dates, drifted through the welter of indecision she'd suffered over whether she'd have the babe at the hospital or at home, before she finally admitted she'd bought some new nightdresses last time she'd been on the mainland but, no, hadn't exactly packed anything for hospital.

David walked behind them, watching the way Rowena moved, wondering how the human psyche worked, that he could be thinking how attractive she was while his world was falling apart. His next patient was helping himself to a glass of water from the fountain in the corner.

David recognised him with a feeling of relief.

'Ted. I didn't know you were on the list for today. What brings you here?'

He crossed the room to shake hands with his friend, then led him back to the consulting room.

Ted drained the small paper cup and tossed it into David's waste-paper basket. He ignored the chair David offered and did a turn around the room, showing sufficient agitation for David to forget a little about his own problems while he worried about Ted's.

'Actually, I didn't think you'd be here,' Ted finally admitted.

'You didn't want to see me about a medical problem? You'd prefer to see a woman?'

'No way—not for me, mate,' Ted assured him, then he added, 'It's Kelly.' He turned and paced one more length before finally deciding he could do this sitting down.

David propped himself against the desk and waited.

'I think she's sick of the island—well, I hope it's the

island and not me. She's restless and not herself at all. Not unhappy if you gauge unhappiness on tears—she doesn't sit around and cry all day. It's more like she's distracted. As if she's distancing herself from me, and I can't seem to get her back.'

David pictured Kelly Withers in his mind—saw the rich dark red hair flowing in waves across her shoulders, and the bright, red-brown eyes which sparkled with wit and wisdom.

'Kelly unhappy?' It seemed impossible. 'Why now? Has something happened recently? Something changed in your lives?'

Ted shook his head.

'Nothing! We're doing well, we didn't suffer any damage in the fires, the eco tours Kelly's been running kept her busy through summer, and the plans for next season's tours are under way. She's thinking of including Barrett's Beach but, though she usually gets excited about the new plans, even that's not giving her much pleasure.'

He paused, then said in a doom-laden voice, 'I think she's fed up with the island. People get that way, you know. Especially city-bred folk like Kelly.'

'Nonsense!' David said. 'I'm city-bred, yet after three years I can't imagine living anywhere else.'

Though I may have to after this, common sense reminded him. But Ted was seriously rattled, which was enough to concern David about the situation. Sufficient, even, to divert at least part of his mind from his huge personal problems.

'I thought a woman doctor might have some insight into what's happening with Kelly,' Ted added lamely.

'Not without seeing the patient,' David told him. 'It's OK for you to come in and lay the groundwork, but how were you going to get Kelly here?'

Ted lifted his broad shoulders in a heavy shrug.

'I hadn't figured out the next move. In fact, I knew you and this Sarah were friends, so I'd thought maybe...'

'We could do it socially? Sunday afternoon barbecue at the Withers'?'

'Something like that,' Ted admitted.

'We could probably still do it but you'd be better off talking to Kelly. She'd kill you if she found out you'd set this up behind her back. Talk to the woman, ask her what's wrong.'

'You ever tried that with a woman?' Ted asked. 'First they say, "nothing", in a voice that suggests it's far worse than you imagined, then if you persist they launch into the kind of explanation Freud himself would have found frightening, losing you about the fourth sentence so you haven't a clue what they're talking about, though you're fairly sure it's all your fault.'

David found himself smiling.

'Kelly's not like that,' he protested. 'In fact, I've rarely met a person, male or female, more able to speak her mind. She wasn't selected as head of the island's tourism board for nothing.'

'Well, she's changed!' Ted said forcefully.

'Physically, is she well? I mean, does she look well? Or is she tired, run down? Couldn't you persuade her to see a doctor? Sarah should be here tomorrow...'

He didn't feel any different, but something must have shown in his face as his mind flashed back to where Sarah was now, for Ted stood up again and reached out to clasp his shoulder, muttering an oath against his own stupidity at the same time.

'Here I am, blathering on, and you're obviously out of it yourself. Rough night with a patient? Some tragedy that hasn't hit the gossip lines yet?'

David rubbed his hands across his face.

'You'll hear soon enough. Sue-Ellen's body has been found.'

'Out at the farm? At your place?'

David gave a huff of helpless mirth.

'Where else?' he said, shaking his head in a weary denial of the impossible fact. 'It's as if some malign fate is determined I'll never be happy again!'

'Nonsense!' Ted repudiated this gloomy assumption, then swore to himself, adding aloud, 'Oh, man! I'm so sorry! Sorry I ever got you involved with the Merlyn family! But for you to have to go through this! Where was she? Had she fallen somewhere? Down a well? Did the place have wells?'

Ted was thinking about accidents—which David himself had assumed when Sue-Ellen had disappeared. But he could no longer hide behind such a contrarily comforting thought.

'She was in a trunk—it has to be murder.'

Ted's fingers tightened on his shoulder.

'David! Oh, mate! What can I say? But you shouldn't be here, listening to people tell their tales of woe. You've said yourself people mostly want reassurance, not doctoring, so go home—let their wives or husbands, their mothers, anyone else, reassure them.'

'I'm better off at work,' David told him. 'Though once word gets out I probably won't even have that to cling to.'

'Nonsense. Islanders judge people for themselves. They'd already decided you were an innocent party in Sue-Ellen's disappearance long before you came back here to practise. In fact, they found your return quite touching—as if you needed to be close to your memories of her.'

David considered this for a moment. He'd given up paediatrics and left the city because the gossip had hurt and saddened him, but he'd never fully analysed his reasons for choosing Three Ships as his future home.

He'd simply come.

'Close to where the happy memories were, perhaps,' he told Ted. 'Back when I came over for a holiday at your place and first met Sue-Ellen. I thought she was the most beautiful thing I'd ever seen—the most precious. Like a Dresden figurine.'

'But tough as teak beneath the fragile beauty,' Ted put in. 'I imagine you discovered that somewhere along the way.'

'Like on our honeymoon!' David admitted. 'She was flabbergasted to think I'd expected her to ski on a skiing holiday. Soon put *me* right.'

'I tried to tell you,' Ted reminded him. 'Lovely to look at but lethal as hell, both those girls—or women, I should say. They matured very young—knew all the tricks to drive a man wild. Leading him on then turning away. I dated Mary-Ellen—though I was never entirely sure which one I was going out with—one summer when I was still at school. I thought I'd die from the pain she caused with her teasing.'

'But, whatever they were, it doesn't alter the fact Sue-Ellen's dead,' David said. 'And no one has the right to take another person's life. No one had the right to deny Sue-Ellen her life. *Especially* not Sue-Ellen, who was so essentially alive, if you know what I mean.'

'You're not talking like a murderer,' Ted said, homing in on the real problem with a friend's accuracy.

'I've never thought or acted like one either,' David assured him, 'though I doubt many people will believe it. I'm afraid it's going to be hard to prove I didn't do it—and without proof people will make up their own minds.'

Ted gave him a little shake.

'In your favour! OK, the proof might be hard to come by, but the islanders'll stand by you. They judge the person they know, not what they hear about him.'

'Oh, come on!' David said, but he smiled, albeit grimly. 'The islanders are just the same as people everywhere. They'll roll out all the clichés like ''There's no smoke without fire'' and discuss it ad nauseam, at the same time casting dubious glances my way to see if somehow I've developed a mark of Cain.'

Ted made a muted noise of disagreement, but David knew he was right. Unless whoever had killed Sue-Ellen was found, his life on the island was over.

And just as dead as his lost wife were his hopes of wooing and winning Rowena.

Which reminded him, he'd promised Margo he'd contact Barry.

Beyond the window he could see kids coming home from school, shoving each other and laughing.

How could everyday life go on as if nothing had happened? Was personal disaster so insignificant it had no effect on the rest of the world?

'Let's consider a physical cause first, as far as Kelly is concerned. Talk her into coming in to see Sarah. Tell her you're concerned about her health, that you think she's doing too much, and ask her to come for your sake—just to set your mind at rest.'

'I'll try,' Ted said, sighing deeply, but whether over the problem of getting his wife to a doctor or David's tenuous hold on islander loyalty, David couldn't tell.

He saw Ted out, greeted Mrs Smythe, one of the island's two centenarians, then glanced up as the doorbell tinkled again. His heart did its lurching thing as Rowena walked in. Obviously the brain and heart must operate on different wavelengths where emotions were concerned. Far from disappearing, the physical manifestations of his attraction to Rowena seemed, if anything, to have increased in strength.

She smiled at him, making things worse internally, and murmured, 'When you've seen Mrs Smythe, maybe you could pop across to the hospital. Barry's already there, but no one's told him about Margo yet. He'll probably be more panicky than her and, as there could be another twelve to eighteen hours before Junior Ryan arrives, I thought he might be best left in ignorance for a short time, anyway.'

She paused, then went on, 'And it turns out Nell's on the mainland, due back on tomorrow's flight, if it comes, so it looks like you'll be it as far as the delivery is concerned.'

'Me? Both the sisters at the hospital can deliver babies, so can you—you've had the training and must have done some prac. work when you trained.'

'A hundred years ago!' Rowena said, exaggerating tenfold. 'And anyway, I don't think Margo would be happy with any of us. As far as she's concerned, it's Nell or you—preferably both!'

'Margo's at the hospital?' David asked, but although the conversation must have seemed quite normal to Rowena, and no doubt to Mrs Smythe had she been able to hear it, to him it seemed unbelievable—removed to a distance by the thoughts churning in his head.

Foremost of which was how he felt about the woman to whom he was talking, how precious she'd suddenly become to him, how attractive her tall, lissom figure, the long blonde hair casually pulled back into its customary loose knot at the nape of her neck. But jostling attraction from centre stage was the desire to protect her, to distance her from all of this—or himself from her lest he taint her with its mire.

Then, of course, were the even more unwelcome thoughts. Barry's presence at the hospital meant Sarah must also be there—with a trunk and the pitiful remains of what had once been a vital, vibrant woman.

A woman he had loved, then lost, even before she'd disappeared.

'I'll see Mrs Smythe then pop across. Who else is on the list? Can you remember?'

'Sally Jenkins—young Harry's second lot of shots. I'll phone her and ask her to come tomorrow instead. If I can't get hold of her, I'll do the immunisation and she can see you about any other problems or worries she might have some other time.'

'Bless you,' David said, and he smiled at her, though he knew he shouldn't because smiles drew people closer, and he was supposed to be doing a distancing thing!

Rowena carried the smile with her as she turned away. She tucked it into the cold place in her heart where the previous evening's rejection had turned heat to ice in a split second. Felt the arrival of the smile thaw a little of the ice.

Behind her, David was helping Mrs Smythe to her feet and supporting her arm as she headed, in her slightly tipsy fashion, towards the consulting room.

Like the Carters, Mrs Smythe would have come to check out the new doctor so she, too, would be disappointed. Normally, David went to see her when she needed a consultation, while a roster of women, including Rowena, called on a daily basis to see to her housekeeping and shopping.

'Tough!' Rowena murmured to herself, then was dismayed at the lack of sympathy in her reaction.

But this afternoon, the inquisitiveness of the local population seemed irritating, while imagining how they'd react to the news of Sue-Ellen's murder made Rowena's stomach churn.

CHAPTER FIVE

SARAH drove back to town in David's car, following the police vehicle to the hospital. She had to admire the way Barry handled things, backing up close to the small building behind the hospital, sending the constable for the key, then the two policemen lifting the trunk, now loosely covered by a tarpaulin, straight through the door so there was minimum exposure to anyone who might have been about.

With a tightening of her gut, Sarah followed, telling herself it didn't matter who it was—all she had to do was document her findings. She parked to the right of the building, between it and the hospital, so the car was in the shade.

The room had a stark look of abandonment and the accompanying echoes of despair, though it was clean enough and equipped with a small table on which the two men had placed the trunk, a stainless-steel dissecting table, a bench against one wall, deep sinks and taps, one with a hose already attached, and a tired-looking metal folding chair.

'I've a sheet of plastic in the trunk. Nick, you know where it is. Fetch it, would you? Then pop into the hospital and let Jane know we're here so she doesn't think the place is being invaded. After that, you can go back and mind the shop in case a crime wave breaks out on the island.'

The young policeman departed—eagerly! Glad to be out of the place, no doubt. Although some young constables were excited by the novelty, and here on the island, Sarah imagined, anything would serve to break the monotony.

He returned to hand a flat plastic bag to Barry, then dutifully withdrew.

Barry opened the sealed bag and pulled out a folded sheet of plastic.

'They give us all this stuff for use in and around crime scenes, but I've never had much need of it,' he said. 'Never even had to dust for fingertips since I've been here, because if you see young Aaron West disappearing through someone's bathroom window, you don't have far to look for a suspect when something goes missing. Mind you, that time he was going in because Mrs Ross had locked her keys inside, but you get to know who nicks what and they'll usually tell you if you ask.'

He was talking to ease his own tension, Sarah guessed, but she didn't mind as it was helping her as well. Together they spread the plastic on the stainless-steel trolley. As Sarah looked around to see what was available in the way of equipment, Jane Ross, the senior sister at the hospital, appeared.

'What do you need?' she asked, addressing her question to Sarah but glancing curiously at the trunk. 'I don't keep anything out here as the room is a bit damp and things go musty.'

'Right now,' Sarah told her, 'I'd like gowns, plastic aprons, a small tape-recorder, if you happen to have such a thing, tapes, paper and pens. Goggles, masks, gloves—plenty of them. I want Barry to give me a hand in a minute and we'll need to be double-gloved. Tongs and tweezers. Specimen jars.'

Jane departed, a far-away look in her eyes suggesting that she was mentally repeating Sarah's list.

'I assume you have both paper and plastic evidence bags,' Sarah said to Barry. 'I don't want to disturb anything I don't have to, but if you need to see it's all there, she'll have to come out, and I'll need to bag any clothes we take off her.'

Her companion made a noise signifying agreement, but Sarah guessed he'd rather be anywhere but here.

Though the smell wasn't as bad as that of a body found after a few days. Insects must have found their way inside the trunk at some stage, but they'd left when satisfied and the dry air of the island summer, and the good ventilation in the shed, had dried out what was left.

Or most of it.

Jane returned from her foray into the hospital stock cupboards, pushing a trolley-load of equipment, including, Sarah was pleased to see, gowns, gloves, plastic aprons and a full face mask of clear plastic.

'We had boots somewhere, but I can't find them. I've sent the yardman up to the hardware shop to get a pair of wellies for you.'

She hesitated, her hands on the trolley.

'Do you need an assistant?' she asked, then, before Sarah could reply, continued, 'As the senior on duty, I'd help you myself, but we've just got a midwifery patient in and I'll need to be on hand for her.'

She glanced uneasily towards Barry, who'd returned with a couple of packs of evidence bags, then kept talking.

'If you need someone, Rowena's done this before. Once in a storm when a young man died unexpectedly and Peter, her husband who was the doctor here, did an autopsy. There are probably other times as well, which I can't remember.'

Sarah considered all the information.

'I might need someone,' she said, then she, too, glanced at Barry. 'Unless you'd like to assist—you'll be here anyway.'

The look of horror on Barry's face was enough to tell her what he thought of that idea, although most of the help Sarah needed would be photographic.

'OK, could you phone Rowena, and ask her if she'd be willing to help? If so, she could come right over.'

Jane slipped away again.

'Have you got a good camera, apart from the Polaroid?' Sarah asked Barry.

'Sure! I'll get Nick to bring it down.'

He eased towards the door, but Sarah caught him before he escaped.

'You've already got shots of her in the trunk, but I want to take more when she's out, so how about you give me a hand before you go?'

He came reluctantly forward, accepting the gown, apron, gloves and mask, then pulling the things on over his clothes, all the while grumbling under his breath. From the gist of it, his complaints were more against a policeman's lot, rather than Sarah's request for assistance.

She started the tape-recorder so she could tape what she was doing. Later, when she wrote up her notes, she'd use the tape rather than rely on her memory.

Then, with Barry's help, Sarah, now also gloved and gowned and aproned, eased the skeletal remains out. Some joints, no doubt tastier to the insects than others, collapsed immediately; the clothes, as Sarah had suspected, disintegrated when touched. Bones, dust and drops of moisture from beneath the body dropped onto the plastic. As soon as the skeleton was safely on the sheet, Barry stepped away.

'I'll leave the rest up to you,' he told Sarah, backing towards the door, the green hue of his face suggesting he needed to get out fast. Sarah heard a murmur of voices outside, then Barry's deep bass, sounding upset. She ignored them, using tweezers to extract the remaining bones from the trunk.

The door opened behind her and someone came in—two someones from the murmur of conversation.

Rowena?

She tweezered up another bone. Small bones of either the foot or the hand—hard to tell until she'd cleaned them up and set them in place with the rest of the skeleton. More conversation behind her, and when Rowena didn't materialise nearby Sarah glanced around, to see the young policeman and David standing there.

'Barry's wife is having very early labour pains,' David

explained. 'He's popped into the hospital to see her while Nick makes sure you don't throw anything away.'

He spoke lightly but his voice was so strained Sarah wondered he could speak at all.

Then Rowena walked through the door and the agony on David's face seemed to intensify. But when she reached out to touch his arm, he shifted so her hand met air, then fell helplessly by her side.

'You wanted an assistant?' she said to Sarah, stepping forward into the light which revealed new lines etched into her clear, tanned skin. Lines of inner suffering—and perhaps fear.

'Gowns and gloves first,' Sarah told her. 'And a mask across your mouth and nose, and goggles over your eyes. Otherwise, if I drop a bit and something splashes up, you'd be vulnerable. No! Actually, hold the gowns and gloves for the moment. Right now I need you to take photos.'

'I've got the camera,' Nick said, holding up a professional-looking bag. 'Spare film and all.'

He still had the Polaroid camera in a bag slung across his shoulder, so looked like a newspaper cameraman who'd strayed into the wrong place.

Without being asked, Rowena took the second bag and unzipped the cover to check it out, while Sarah continued with collecting the detritus from the bottom of the trunk.

'Photograph everything,' she said to her helper. 'The trunk, the skeleton, the little bones. But make sure you write down each shot you take. Is it a new film?'

Rowena checked the camera.

'Yes, the number counter shows number one, but I'll need a pencil and paper.' She looked around, searching through the items on the trolley.

'OK,' she told the doctor. 'I'm all set. I'll put date and time then write down what each shot is and where I've taken it from.'

Behind her, she could feel David's stillness, only she

knew it shouldn't be possible to *feel* stillness. Perhaps it was pain she could feel—the same kind of pain which had taken up residence in her heart.

He'd moved away from her earlier, as though her touch might contaminate him, but his agony was so evident she ached to hold him and offer whatever comfort he would accept.

Sarah was removing small bones and setting them on the plastic at one end of the table, so Rowena began her photographic work, first focussing on the still folded skeleton. The young policeman followed her, snapping off shots, not one to one with her but often enough, then waiting for the paper to slide out of the camera before setting each print on the bench to dry.

And he, too, was writing down his shots, scribbling in his little notebook as if his life depended on it.

Rowena found him distracting, though she knew it probably wasn't him bothering her but David, standing so still just inside the door.

Shot one—the body taken from inside the doorway, four feet away, she wrote. Second shot taken to the right of shot one and closer, maybe two feet, from the body.

She scribbled the words then refocussed the camera, wishing she could twist a dial and refocus her mind. Tune out her own—and David's—fear and confusion.

Third shot...

She moved around the table and when Sarah declared she had the lot, Rowena photographed the collection of small bones.

'I'm going to stretch her out after I've removed the remnants of her clothing.'

Speaking quietly into the tape-recorder, Sarah shifted the skeleton so it lay on its back, then gently eased the legs into an extended position. Dry sinews cracked and popped like arthritic joints and soon the unfortunate woman lay stretched out on the table, shabby scraps of denim jeans defining the sharp edge of the tibia in each lower leg, shreds of a green and blue checked shirt clinging to her chest, delineating the ribcage.

Rowena had gone right around the room so was back on the side by the door, just in front of David and Nick, when Sarah, handling a fresh pair of tweezers with infinite care, lifted the first strip of material off the woman's right leg.

Rowena heard David's gasp and spun towards him, in time to see him reach out to the wall for support.

Lowering the camera, she stepped towards him, aware that Nick was already offering physical support.

'Hold the camera,' she said brusquely to the younger man, then she hooked the only chair in the room forward with one foot and steered David's limp form towards it.

'Get your head down,' she ordered. 'We certainly wouldn't be able to support you if you pass right out.'

He obeyed, dropping his head down almost to his knees, breathing deeply to replenish the oxygen supply to his brain.

She knelt beside him, feeling his forehead, wondering if fever might explain the sudden collapse. But his forehead was cool, and the hand that touched her on the arm was icy cold.

'What is it? What upset you?'

'Nothing!'

His denial was too abrupt to be believed and he must have heard the harshness in the word for he added more gently, 'I'm all right now.' But when she saw the eyes he raised to hers, she knew he was so far from all right he might never find the way back.

'You shouldn't be here,' she whispered crossly. 'It's probably not even legal to have you looking on. What happened?'

He shook his head, denying anything more catastrophic had occurred, but Rowena knew he'd been holding up well until Sarah had removed the scrap of cloth from his wife's skeletal leg.

Was it the cloth? What she was wearing? Could that have upset him?

She stood up and looked again at the woman laid out on the plastic, seeking an explanation. Was there a scar, a mark, a tattoo?

Sue-Ellen marring her beautiful, pampered skin with a tattoo? Hardly! And there wasn't enough skin for a scar or a tattoo to be obvious.

But there *was* an anklet. A fine gold chain, fastened with a heart-shaped lock.

Rowena felt her heart contract into a small hard ball. He'd come to see Sarah work, still hoping in the depths of his being it wouldn't be his wife. Then the anklet had confirmed it.

No doubt, it was a present he'd given her—given her with all the love the heart-shaped clasp implied.

Rowena felt as if her heart had cracked open and the blood was seeping out, leaving her feeling cold and shaky.

'Where's my photographer?' Sarah asked, and Rowena knew she had to at least act normally. Heaven knew, she'd had enough 'acting normal' practice after Peter and Adrian had disappeared. Surely she could do it again.

Taking the camera from Nick, she returned to her duties, focussing on the anklet as Sarah pointed to it and spoke to record its presence on the tape. Rowena knew she was probably taking more photographs of leg bones than Sarah would need, but concentrating on what she was doing helped with the pretence.

David had read about denial, but hadn't realised before today just how real the state was. Perhaps the blonde hair had started it, started him thinking the body could be that of some other small woman—after all, it was impossible to identify the remains by sight. So he'd watched and waited, though for what he hadn't known. Perhaps some miracle to prove this wasn't Sue-Ellen, that she wasn't dead and hadn't been lying hidden in the shed all this time?

The very thought had made him feel ill—so ill the knowledge that once again he'd be the focus of a murder investigation hadn't bothered him at all.

Except as far as it might affect his friends.

And ruin any chance he might ever have had of forming a relationship with Rowena.

The pain of that idea had helped the denial—it wouldn't be Sue-Ellen. It would be a stranger. So many women wore jeans and checked shirts.

Then he saw the chain and remembered how she'd flaunted it at him! Teasing him about the new admirer—lover?—who'd bestowed it on her, fastening it himself with some kind of unopenable lock. It would have to be cut off, she'd told him, should she ever wish to remove it!

Which she didn't! Or so she'd said, only days before Mary-Ellen had come back from Austria and Sue had gone to meet her, then stayed on with her sister in the old family home—catching up, Sue-Ellen had said.

To consider leaving him, that was how the gossips had seen it—and later the police had taken the same view. They hadn't known Sue-Ellen's pleasure came from taunting people—from seeing them suffer—so there'd have been no fun in simply leaving him. Not straight away!

He studied the anklet again while all hope that the body on the table might not be his wife fled. Only Rowena's prompt action saved him slumping full length on the floor and making a complete fool of himself. Now here he was, crouched on the chair with his body shaking so much he didn't dare try to stand, while his head battled to get around what was going on.

Behind him, the door opened, and he noticed vaguely that it was Jane.

'David, can you come?' the nursing sister asked. 'Margo's perfectly well, but she's hysterical and Barry's only making her worse. I'm wondering if there's any sedative we can give at this early stage to calm her down, something that won't stop the natural progression of her labour.'

He looked up at Jane, hearing the words, even processing them, but wondering if he'd be able to function normally. She wanted *him* to reassure someone?

Of course you will, his sterner self told him. It's shock manifesting itself. Natural enough in the circumstances.

He stood up—shakily, but he got there—then he smiled reassuringly at Rowena who'd stopped taking photos long enough to look anxiously towards him.

Remembered he shouldn't be smiling at Rowena so he frowned instead, then wanted to apologise as he saw her own tentative smile fade to disappointment.

Hell, but he was making a hash of things at the moment.

He reached the door—a whole two paces away—and was going out when Sarah called to him.

'And don't come back,' she told him. 'I'll be busy here for a few hours so you'll have to hold the fort. Get yourself some food and, if you're not needed by patients, have a rest. Accept you've had a shock and treat your body accordingly.'

It was safe to smile at Sarah, so he allowed himself a real one.

'Yes, Mum!' he said, and saw her eyes glimmer behind the mask.

But it was the memory of Rowena's eyes he took with him from the room, their grey depths so full of concern and compassion he almost forgot about protecting her from whatever flak might be coming his way and nearly hurled himself into her arms.

Rowena watched him go, then following instructions from Sarah, set the camera on the bench and donned gown, apron, gloves, mask and goggles.

'I've set all the remnants of clothing aside for the moment. We'll bag them and label them later.'

'Why are the clothes in such poor condition? I've clothes and sheets that have been stored away in trunks for years, but they haven't disintegrated.'

'Bodies have a whole host of bacteria in them, and this bacteria starts the process of decay. I imagine, as the body decays, the fluids permeate the cloth which in turn degenerates. Then, if you get insect infestation, and they attack the edible bits that have seeped into the material, it further weakens it.'

Sarah looked up and grinned at her.

'I'm not a forensic scientist so that's guesswork, not fact,' she warned. 'Now, you've got shots of the body without the clothes?'

'Probably too many,' Rowena replied, though she was wondering where David was, and how he was faring. It was impossible to imagine how he might feel! 'I had to load another film,' she added, responding diligently to Sarah in an effort to calm the jitters in her heart.

'There can't be too many,' Sarah assured her. 'The people in the city can always throw away anything they don't want. By rights we should X-ray her so we've X-ray film as well, but I can't see the point when they'll do it again in the city where the proper autopsy will take place.'

'So what *do* we do?' Rowena said. It was better to stay busy. That way she could keep her mind at least partially off David.

'Can you remember all the bones of the hand from your anatomy lessons?' Sarah asked.

'Carpals, metacarpals and phalanges—they're the fingers, right?'

'Exactly,' Sarah told her. 'And the foot's the same only they're tarsals, metatarsals and phalanges in the toes.'

'Can we tell them apart?' Rowena peered dubiously at the pile of small bones Sarah had collected.

'We should be able to,' Sarah assured her. 'Usually, the name denotes the shape so if you take the eight carpal bones you get the scaphoid or boat-shaped—see, here's one.'

Sarah teased at the bone with her tweezers before separating it from the rest.

'Lunate, like the moon,' Rowena remembered from her anatomy lessons. Lunacy has the same derivation and that's where you're headed if you don't put David right out of your mind for the moment and concentrate on what's happening here. 'And there's a triangular as well, isn't there? And in the same row another—I can't think of it.'

'Think of peas,' Sarah reminded her. 'Here...' She teased a small pea-shaped bone free. 'Pisiform. Then in the next row you have the trapezium, trapezoid, capitate and hamate.'

'The trapezoid and trapezium are pretty self-explanatory, but capitate—something to do with heads? And hamate—I haven't a clue. Can't remember at all.'

'The capitate has a slightly swollen head, and the hamate is hook-shaped. See, there are the eight. They might not all be from the same hand but as long as we end up with the right number of bones, Barry will be happy. Can you find matches to each of these while I sort through the phalanges to separate feet from hands?'

Rowena found a pair of tweezers and began to search. They were bones, not bits of a woman David had loved. Not bits of any human—just bones!

What had Sarah said about Barry?

'Why will it make Barry happy?' Rowena asked, keeping her voice low as she didn't want Nick to think she was gossiping.

'Because if we can report that the skeleton's complete, he doesn't have to search for more bones. Also, if you think about it, it might show she wasn't moved into the trunk at a later date. Well, not much later. Moving her a couple of years later could have resulted in the perpetrator losing some of these little bones.'

'The perpetrator!' Rowena echoed, reality smashing through her carefully erected reality-barrier. 'What a truly chilling description!'

'Worse than murderer?' Sarah asked, the rising inflection in the words suggesting surprise.

'I don't know—they're both frightening,' Rowena told her. And neither could possibly apply to David—I know they couldn't. She wanted to yell the words into the air, but the policeman's presence kept her quiet.

Sarah glanced her way, obviously expecting more, and Rowena struggled to regain her poise before replying.

'To me, perpetrator has dreadful connotations of plotting and planning. I could understand, just, someone picking up an axe and doing away with a nagging spouse in the heat of anger, but planning to do away with someone it makes my blood run cold.'

'Doesn't do much good for the victim either,' Sarah joked, and the silly remark eased some of the tension in the room.

Nick had apparently overcome his early nervousness. He'd retrieved the camera Rowena had set down, and was now moving around them, snapping off shots and looking as if he was permanently poised for action.

'Ran out of film for the Polaroid,' he explained, 'and didn't want to go back to the station for more. But I've got the gist of what you want, so I thought I'd keep going. Just tell me if you want something special.'

'Did you get the anklet?' Sarah asked.

'I did earlier,' Rowena told her, while her mind returned to David's reaction to the thin gold chain. Again her heart stuttered in its rhythm, and the heavy ache in her chest intensified. Had she been foolish to think love might be possible between them?

She stared at the anklet, still shiny in places. Could love keep something polished? 'Should we take it off?'

'I think not,' Sarah said slowly, 'but our photos are insurance should it slip off on the journey. There were enough ankle bones in place to keep it there this long, so my guess is that most of these bones are wrist and the long metacarpals and metatarsals, and phalanges. Well, that's not a guess—you can see from the shape.'

Rowena returned to her sorting, concentrating on what she was doing to exclude the other painful thoughts, seeing the collection of bones as a puzzle, like a jigsaw, although the anklet had been so decidedly—so pathetically—personal, it was hard to hold onto impersonal!

'Stop this farce immediately!'

The door burst open and the words erupted into the heavy silence of the small room.

Mary-Ellen had arrived.

'Where's the other policeman?' she demanded, looking at Nick with the kind of disdain a star might reserve for underlings on a movie set.

'He's not here,' Nick said, lowering the camera and practically standing to attention in front of the newcomer.

'And he's left you in charge? Some genius he is!' the little virago stormed. 'Haven't you ever heard of collusion? Or destruction of evidence? Don't you know that woman is David Wright's friend?' She thrust a red-tipped finger towards Sarah. 'And you're letting her touch the body? She could take away whatever she feels might be incriminating. Do anything she likes.'

'No, ma'am,' Nick said carefully. 'That's why I'm here and we've got a photographic record as well.'

'Let me see that camera!' Mary-Ellen snorted.

Nick might have been bemused—perhaps even intimidated—by the woman, but he stood his ground and certainly didn't hand over the camera.

'It's you who shouldn't be here, ma'am,' he said, stepping away from her.

But the movement caused her to shift her ground, and somehow she fell, grasping at his arm as she lost her balance and sending the camera crashing to the ground.

Hard pieces of plastic burst up like fragments of a grenade, and the exposed film unrolled, stretching across the floor like grey ribbon.

'That's destruction of police property,' Sarah said, moving in front of the table to protect the body from any further violence.

'It was an accident!' Mary-Ellen retorted, as Nick helped her back to her feet.

'Yes,' Sarah said, though her voice revealed her doubts about this statement. 'Well, if you've got a problem with the autopsy, address it to me as I'm the one in charge here. The policeman is merely following correct procedure, which, in a case of suspicious death, means not letting the body out of his sight so evidence can't be destroyed.'

Mary-Ellen glared at her.

'You've no right to be doing an autopsy. This place isn't equipped for the job and, besides being far too close to the man responsible for my sister's death, you certainly wouldn't be qualified.'

Sarah, who'd been prepared to give the woman a little leeway, considering the shock she'd suffered earlier, now stiffened her spine and drew her slim body erect, making herself as tall as possible.

'As it happens, I *am* qualified—and experienced—so I'd suggest you leave me here to do my job, under the watchful eyes of the police, of course.'

No need to tell Mary-Ellen she wasn't doing an autopsy but a preliminary examination. She looked beyond the woman to the tall quiet man and felt uneasiness stir in her stomach.

'Do you have any right to be here?' she asked him, but

she'd hardly registered the barely perceptible shake of his head before Mary-Ellen replied.

'Of course he has the right to be here. He's working for me. He's a detective—trained in homicide. He's probably forgotten more than these local yokels would learn in fifty years.'

'If he's working for you, he's private now, and that doesn't give him the right to be here,' Sarah said firmly.

The woman started forward as if to strike at her, but the man caught her arm and murmured something that stopped the headlong rush. But Sarah hadn't been concerned about possible attack, more concerned about the uneasiness within her which had now turned to nausea.

'You said you came to sort through your family belongings,' she said, staring at Mary-Ellen as she tried to make sense of all the implications. 'Why would you bring an experienced homicide detective with you?'

CHAPTER SIX

'BECAUSE your *friend* murdered my sister!' Mary-Ellen snapped. 'I've always known he did, and now I'll be proved right!'

She smiled triumphantly at Sarah, before rounding on Nick, who was kneeling on the concrete floor, carefully collecting bits of the broken camera and torn film and dropping the debris into an evidence bag. He'd even taken the time to pull on gloves, but somehow Sarah couldn't see Barry taking the 'accidental' destruction any further.

'Where's your boss? The other policeman?' she demanded.

'He's inside—in the hospital. His wife's having a baby.'

Mary-Ellen threw up her hands in disgust.

'I don't believe this! You stay right here, and don't let that woman touch my sister again. I'm going to get this nonsense stopped if I have to go to the Premier himself.'

She whirled out of the room as suddenly as she'd whirled into it, leaving the original occupants bemused, while the enigmatic private detective remained where he was, just inside the door.

'Can she stop you?' Rowena asked.

Sarah shook her head.

'I doubt it, though the gentleman could probably tell you for sure.'

She nodded towards the stranger, but Rowena had no intention of speaking to someone who was seeking to do harm to David.

'Don't you know?' She tried Nick this time, but the young man simply set his bag of camera scraps on the bench then turned towards her and shook his head.

'There are all kinds of legal angles to everything a copper does,' he said, 'so I wouldn't like to say for certain what she can or can't do.'

He looked uncertainly at Sarah.

'Are you a *good* friend of David's?'

Rowena saw the flash of anger in Sarah's eyes.

'I hope you're not implying my friendship with David would make any difference to my findings here.'

'No, no, of course not!' The young man backed off. 'I just didn't know. I thought you were probably someone he'd got through an agency or something. Like the force sends a replacement when Barry or I take holidays.'

It was exactly what most people would think, Rowena realised. David hadn't told his patients he was taking leave until Sarah had arrived on the island, when he'd simply introduced her as his locum—the woman who'd be taking over for three weeks.

'How did—?' Rowena began, but a look from Sarah, who had ignored Mary-Ellen's decree and continued sorting bones, silenced her.

Rowena took the hint and turned her attention back to the carpal bones, sifting through the collection and selecting matching pieces one by one. But the question wouldn't go away—so as she sorted and arranged the little bones, her mind chased possible explanations.

The door opened again, and Barry returned, fortunately without Mary-Ellen.

Ignoring the private detective, he spoke to Sarah.

'What do you think?'

'I'm not quite finished sorting these small bones, but I'd be willing to say we'll find it all here.'

'Good!' he said. 'Then as soon as you're done, wrap her up in the plastic and Nick will help you slip the lot into a body bag. We'll bag the trunk as well. Mr Page, I'll allow you to remain where you are as Ms...the lady's representative...seeing as how she's got a...as she's upset over all of this...but you're not to touch anything or move from that spot. Once the doc's all done, this room will be locked and padlocked until either the homicide detectives get here or the body can be taken to the mainland.'

He then ran his hands through his hair and muttered, 'Do you think you can handle things, Nick? I'm having a baby here. I can't be running backwards and forwards all the time to tell you what to do.'

It was an unjust remark, given how good the young man had been, but Sarah realised how uptight Barry must be, and Nick obviously understood, for he grinned at his boss and said, 'I'll try, mate. I really will.'

Sarah worked more quickly now, scanning the body, listing the bones, assuring herself they were all accounted for.

Nick produced a body bag and with Rowena's help he and Sarah wrapped the fragile remains of Sue-Ellen Wright in plastic, then slid the sheath into the thick rubber bag and zipped it up.

By the time they emerged from the room, the silent watcher still with them, it was dark, and the rain that had drummed relentlessly on the tiles above them while they'd worked now whipped around them like icy flails, driven by a wind that had picked up speed as it had crossed thousands of miles of empty ocean.

'Come to my house,' Rowena suggested to Sarah. 'We'll go through the hospital to tell David that's where we'll be. He might want to stay as well. With Margo in labour, he'll be closer to the action.'

They made the dash across the covered walkway to the hospital together, leaving Nick behind to secure the building, and Paul Page to do whatever private investigators were supposed to do.

Perhaps report to his boss—if he could find her!

'Can David go home—if he wanted to?' Rowena asked Sarah. 'I mean, is his house a crime scene? What's happening out there?'

They were on the back veranda of the hospital, dabbing at their damp skin and clothes with towels an aide had provided for them.

'I can't see what harm it could do, him going back. After all this time, what could anyone find? Barry said earlier he didn't want people in the house, but I doubt he could seal off the house as well as the shed. For one thing, all my clothes are out there and, though I'm happy not to be driving far in this weather, I'll need them eventually. And David will need clothes as well.'

'Which a person delegated by our trusty local policeman will go out and collect, though not tonight, I believe.'

David's voice made them both turn, and the statement told them he'd heard at least part of the conversation.

Rowena dropped the towel she'd been using onto a chair and went to him.

'You're going to stay at my place, and don't argue,' she told him. 'In fact, let's all head over there now. I know what we've been doing this afternoon should put anyone off their tucker, but it hasn't worked for me. I'm starving.'

She hoped she'd sounded like the calm, sensible nurse-receptionist he'd come to trust over their years as colleagues, not the erratic in-love female who'd kissed him the previous evening.

But whatever he thought of the invitation, he had little choice but to accept as Sarah added her approval to the scheme.

'Great idea. Let's all go. Who knows when one of us will be called out? So obey the first rule taught to med students. Eat when you can, and sleep when you can.'

'That's two rules,' David told her, but he didn't argue and Rowena felt a pleasurable warmth ease its way into her blood at the thought of having David stay in her house.

For whatever reason!

'Whose car is where?' he asked.

'Yours is here. I parked it just over there,' Sarah responded, pointing through the driving rain to where a barely discernible dark shape hunched beside the outbuilding might, with imagination, be taken for a vehicle.

'Mine's undercover around the far side of the hospital,' Rowena said. 'Let's all go in it so we don't have to get wet again.'

'I'll check on Margo first,' David told her.

'I'll come with you,' Sarah said. 'You can introduce me to her. I'm actually the doctor on duty on this island at the moment so I'm the one who should be on call.'

David gave her a tired smile.

'We'll argue about it later, shall we?'

He led Sarah into the hospital and, watching them go, Rowena wondered again about Mary-Ellen's knowledge of their friendship. Would the sisters have been so close that Sue-Ellen had mentioned David's friend, even though, according to Sarah, the two had never met?

Or had the detective been employed some time ago? Had Mary-Ellen paid him or one of his colleagues, to sift through David's past, searching for any secrets, relentlessly tracking him until yesterday she'd been confident enough to pounce?

The thought of such silent but dogged pursuit made Rowena feel physically ill.

'But it didn't make you suspicious of David,' Sarah pointed out when, much later, they were washing and drying their dinner dishes. It had been dinner for two, as in the end David hadn't returned with them, staying on at the hospital to reassure his expectant patient and her nervous spouse.

'Of course not!' Rowena told her. 'Anyone who knows David couldn't possibly suspect him of killing anyone—particularly someone he loved as much as he loved Sue-Ellen.'

'Has he talked about her a lot?' Sarah asked.

'No. Now I think about it, I doubt he ever has—except

in passing. My wife used to ride, learnt to fly a plane—things like that.'

'Then what makes you think he carries this undying passion for her?'

Rowena remembered what had first made her think it, but 'because he hated me for kissing him in the bedroom they'd shared' didn't seem like an appropriate reply, so she said instead, 'Well, the way he reacted to the anklet, for one thing! He nearly fainted. I thought it must be because, at that moment, he knew for sure it *was* his wife. Perhaps up till then, he'd held this dream in his heart that one day she'd come back. Maybe she'd had amnesia...'

Sarah chuckled and flipped the teatowel at her.

'You read too many romances,' she teased. 'Have you been torturing yourself with these thoughts all along? Convinced David nurtured this undying love and hopeless dreams of Sue-Ellen's eventual return?'

'He came back to the island, didn't he?' Rowena argued. 'Why would he return to Three Ships if not to be near the place where he first met her? Everyone here knew the story. Knew he was staying with Ted Withers for a long weekend, went to a party and fell instantly in love with her.'

'And probably fell almost as instantly out of it again,' Sarah told her. 'David's too loyal a person to talk about his relationships but, reading between the lines of the letters I did get from him, it wasn't joy and sunshine all the way. They were married in the US, when he was in Saint Louis doing further paediatric training, so no one who knew him well saw much of him for ages. They'd been back in Melbourne less than a year when Sue-Ellen disappeared—'

'But if he didn't come to work on Three Ships because of Sue-Ellen,' Rowena interrupted, 'why did he come here? He wasn't an islander.'

Precisely what I'd like to know, Sarah thought, but a sudden rush of wind then the slamming of the front door told them David had returned, and no further speculation could take place.

He stood in the hall and leaned against the door. The storm had not only approached faster than predicted, it had grown in strength and now battered the island with its fury.

And he'd forgotten to get the keys to his car from Sarah so had had to dash through the rain, first to the surgery where he'd stupidly left his raincoat then on to Rowena's house.

Not wanting to drip water through Rowena's house, he'd discarded the raincoat and shoes in the outer porch, and he now stripped off his sodden socks. He felt the dampness in the lower part of his trousers where the raincoat had failed to reach, and decided he'd be better off without them as well.

Which was when the lights went out.

He managed in the darkness, and had them in his hand, wondering where to put them, when a soft light illuminated the gloomy hall.

'Here's a towel, and a lamp. I'll set it down here. Give me your wet things. I've got a fire going in the living room—I'll hang them above it.'

He heard all Rowena's sensible instructions, but they failed to make much imprint on a mind transfixed by the image of the woman who was giving them. She'd unbound her hair, no doubt to dry it, so it fell like shimmering golden cloth around her shoulders, while, in the lamplight, the grey of her eyes appeared to have darkened so he was looking into deep mysterious pools.

She set the lamp down on the hall coatstand and reached out for his clothes, mimicking her movement of the previous evening.

Only this time it was he who caught her arms, he who leaned in and he who pressed his lips to hers.

'Oh, Rowena, I really shouldn't be here,' he murmured helplessly, as his protective instincts duelled with desire, and lost. He dropped the damp clothes and drew her close, absorbing the faint perfume of her hair, feeling the solid strength of her body, bewitched by the magical essence that seemed to emanate from her, enveloping him in its power.

With his resolve further weakened by the traumatic events of the day, he let his lips find hers.

'And I *definitely* shouldn't be kissing you,' he breathed against their softness, then kissed her hungrily, common sense flying out the window as his body sought solace in the sheer physical delight of holding her close.

Damp shirt-tails and wet jockey shorts did little to mask how he was feeling, and Rowena's thudding heart and aching body responded with a fierceness that suggested it was time for her as well.

Leaving the lamp burning, the wet clothes on the floor and a guest in her living room, she steered David through the door behind him and into the bedroom she'd shared with Peter.

And had never expected to share with another man!

'Rowena!'

The word, her name, was rough with passion, but a question lingered in it. She answered with her kiss, and with her body pressing even closer to his, letting it speak for her, letting her hands and kisses tell him, seduce him. She knew his exhaustion had diminished his will-power but with all her heart she wanted to comfort him in the only way she knew. Ignoring his muttered objections, she used skills she'd forgotten she had, bringing him to such a peak of desire he stopped arguing, and together they fumbled out of their clothes and fell into the downy comfort of the bed.

Murmured sounds, too inarticulate to be called words, whispered from his lips and Rowena felt her skin becoming alert to every movement of the man she'd grown to love so dearly. She spread her fingers across his back, slid them to his hips, feeling the ridge of bone, the tight muscles. His fingers carried on their own tactile exploration, one hand on her breast, one between her thighs, feeling her warmth—her excitement.

She sensed him withdrawing into himself, heard her name uttered in a kind of protest, and once again took command, touching and teasing him until whatever scruples he'd failed to voice were overcome by his desire.

But though his need was as urgent as hers, he didn't hurry, teasing her in turn until she wanted to cry out for release. He must have known, for he entered her, filling all the emptiness she hadn't realised she'd been feeling, bringing the physical side of her to life with a wondrous explosion of sensation and an inner ecstasy that left her shaken and exhausted.

Afterwards, when she felt him grow heavy in her arms, she eased away from him, knowing he'd sleep.

Knowing she wouldn't—at least not for a while.

And not in here. She didn't want to see any regret in his eyes when he woke—and definitely didn't want them to repeat the very pleasurable experience in the hazy warmth of just waking—when the brain would still be slumbering but the bodies remembering enough to want more.

Next time, if there was a next time, it would be in the full knowledge of what they were doing, for both of them.

She gathered up her clothes and crept out of the room, pausing in the hall to pull them on and button herself into some semblance of order. Now all she had to do was face Sarah—the guest she'd deserted halfway through the washing-up!

The light from the fire revealed an empty living room, but the lamp Rowena had left in the kitchen was gone and noises from the bathroom suggested that Sarah was taking a bath.

Damn! I should have got more clothes from my bedroom while I was in there, Rowena realised. She walked back, left the lamp in the hall once again while she opened the door and tiptoed inside, finding by feel a warm nightdress for Sarah and another for herself. Then, remembering Margo in labour at the hospital, she grabbed a handful of underwear, a couple of shirts and a clean pair of jeans.

Perhaps if she offered appropriate clothes, Sarah would go over to the hospital next and let David have a decent sleep.

David! The name sang like a simple melody in her head while the thought of him sleeping right there in her bed sent a slow shiver down her spine. Fighting a desire to touch him, she tiptoed out again.

She knocked lightly on the bathroom door.

'I've a warm nightdress you can borrow, and I found some clean dry clothes. My things will be a bit big for you but they should do.'

The door opened and Sarah, wrapped in a towel, her skin pink from the bath, smiled at her.

'I thought that's probably what you were doing,' she said, the teasing grin lighting little gleams in her eyes. 'And in the dark as well. Thank you!'

She took the clothes then leaned forward and kissed Rowena on the cheek before stepping back and closing the door again.

Must be something to do with passing clothes from one person to another, Rowena decided, pressing her hands to her feverish face.

She went back to the front door and found David's wet clothes on the floor. She took them through and hung them on a drying rack near the fireplace, then went back to get his shoes from outside to stuff with old newspaper then set them to dry as well.

Sarah came in as she finished this task, wearing the nightdress but carrying the other clothing.

'I assume it was David who came in,' she said.

Rowena felt her face flame again and hoped Sarah would blame the heat of the fire.

'Yes, he's gone to sleep.'

'Good!' Sarah told her. 'Best thing for him. We'll let him stay that way. I'll go across to the hospital if anyone's needed, though how will they let you know? I left my mobile at the surgery so I took the liberty of borrowing your phone to ring Tony, but the line was dead.'

'It happens in a storm,' Rowena told her. 'But we've a two-way system that works between places on the island. Knowing David's staying here, whoever's on duty will use the two-way to contact him.'

'Is it in the bedroom? Will it wake him if it suddenly sparks to life?'

Was Sarah aware of Rowena's jittery happiness that she was keeping the conversation focussed on practical matters? Or was she simply trying to ease over an awkward situation with talk?

'It's in the kitchen,' Rowena replied, realising that, whatever Sarah's motive, it was working. 'I'll hear it from the spare bedroom and wake you. I hope you don't mind sharing the bedroom with me. And although the hospital's only across the road and up one, opposite the surgery, you should take my car if you have to go. You can get out under cover at the hospital so you won't get wet. David walked back earlier and got drenched. I'll fit you out with wet-weather gear in case you're called out to anyone else during the night.'

She was talking too much, a sure sign of nervousness, but Sarah didn't seem to notice, picking up instead on one word right near the end of the garbled reply.

'*If* I'm called out? I gathered from Barry's panic that the baby was almost with us.'

Rowena chuckled.

'Didn't you meet Margo? Or was she asleep when you saw her? If you think Barry's bad, Margo's ten times worse.'

'She did seem a little hyper,' Sarah said. 'I thought she

must have been having a contraction at the time I was introduced and put the drama down to that.'

'Well, she might have been,' Rowena said, giving Margo the benefit of the doubt, 'but when David saw her at the surgery she'd just had her first pain. I went home with her to pack, took her up to the hospital and stayed with her for quite a while. I reckon I was with her for an hour at least and there was no further pain so she still had a long time to go before things got interesting.'

'She went to hospital after the first pain?' Sarah sounded as surprised as Rowena had been when Margo had insisted on being admitted immediately.

'She's a panicky type,' Rowena explained.

'Poor thing—she'll be bored to death. Much better to stay home and do things right up to the last minute. In fact, with Braxton-Hicks' contractions, you can ease them by walking, by keeping moving.'

Rowena grinned at her.

'You know that and I know that, but Margo doesn't— nor did she believe it when I told her. Though I doubt she'll be bored. More likely driving the nurse on duty to distraction with demands for this and that.'

'Including demands to see the doctor. Maybe I'd better get out of this very comfortable night attire and into your dry jeans. I'll give it another hour then go over and check on her before going to bed. Surely by then I'll be able to give her some idea of how long it will be and maybe we'll all get some sleep.'

Leaving Sarah in front of the fire, Rowena busied herself with preparations for a night—possibly more than one night—without power. In the storeroom behind the house she checked she had fuel for the generator. If power wasn't restored by morning, she'd run it while she was at work to ensure the frozen things in her refrigerator stayed frozen.

While there, she found a long oilskin that had been

Peter's. She'd put it in the car in case Sarah was called out to somewhere beyond the hospital.

Another couple of lamps might come in handy if they were going to be without power for a few days. And another torch—good. She had new batteries in the kitchen.

Practical Rowena! her brain mocked, but all the time she was fussing over her preparations her physical self was remembering the feel of David's skin, the hungry way his mouth had claimed hers and finally the fierce possession when he'd stopped arguing with himself and given into the dictates and demands of his body.

Her body shivered with remembered delight, then renewed desire warmed it once again.

Would it be so terrible to spend the night with him? Steal some solace from this miserable situation?

Sarah would understand...

Then Rowena recalled the coldness in David's eyes when he'd asked her to leave his bedroom the previous evening, and knew she couldn't handle seeing such a look again.

But could he have made love to her with such passion if he felt nothing? If the coldness had been real?

Perhaps their love-making had been no more than a physical release of tension on his part?

There were no answers to these, or any other of the myriad questions racing through her head.

Practical Rowena reasserted herself.

'Here's a torch to take with you and I'll leave a lamp burning in the garage,' she told Sarah, who was now ready to go across to the hospital. 'You know where the bedroom is. If I go to bed, I'll leave a lamp burning there as well. I've put an oilskin in the car in case you're called out anywhere beyond the hospital, though hopefully you won't be.'

She looked at Sarah's slight frame and shook her head.

'Bad enough the jeans are swimming on you, without you drowning in Peter's oilskin. I know. I'll get David's from the porch—it'll be closer to your size. I can leave

Peter's there for him should he need to go out again. I'd lend you mine but it's got a huge rip down the back from an argument with a barbed-wire fence. I've been meaning to have it patched, so it serves me right if I get wet.'

She walked through the house, pausing in her bedroom doorway to listen to David's quiet, steady breathing. Smiling with memories of the happiness she knew would probably prove transient.

Opening the front door, she fought against the wind, but held it long enough to snag the coat and drag it inside. The porch was deep, its wall protected from the rain, and most of the water collected earlier should have dripped off the coat, though the weight of it suggested it was still fairly damp. Folding it inside out, she took it out to the car, retrieving Peter's and taking it out to the porch where David, if he woke and wanted to go out, would find it.

She watched Sarah back out, then stood in the doorway and saw the headlights illuminating the slashing rain as she drove slowly over to the hospital.

Now, alone, Rowena was tempted to go back into her bedroom but realised an urge to watch her boss sleeping could be considered slightly sick, so she headed for the bathroom where she showered, cleaned her teeth and pulled on her own warm nightgown.

Hardly glamorous attire for the morning after, her mind teased, but her body was still hungover with happiness and ignored the jibe.

As she slipped between the sheets in the room that had once been Adrian's, she felt the familiar stab of pain evoking his name always caused. But life moved on, and while he and Peter would live for ever in her heart and hold a very special place, like a secret shrine, in her memory, she knew she had so much love banked up inside her it would be wrong not to at least offer some of it to David.

* * *

David woke to a greyness which suggested that somewhere beyond the rain and a thick covering of cloud the sun was rising.

He looked around the unfamiliar room, seeking to make form of the shadows, seeking also the answer to what he was doing here.

Rowena's house.

He closed his eyes.

Rowena's bed!

His mind, no doubt refreshed by deep and dreamless sleep, thoughtfully provided an almost complete recollection of his arrival at the house and the events that had followed.

He couldn't recall every word they'd spoken—in fact, couldn't recall any conversation at all—but he was fairly certain he'd fallen on Rowena like a ravening animal, swept her into this room—into this bed—and…

Into this startling picture came sound bites, little murmurs of encouragement, breathy cries of pleasure.

Maybe he hadn't been the ravening animal he'd first supposed. And maybe the pleasure which his body remembered quite vividly had been mutual.

Then why wasn't she here? Snuggled up beside him?

The thought made him sit up. He slammed his hand against his forehead.

Idiot! Halfwit! For Pete's sake, can't you keep a thought in your head for longer than a couple of hours? You're supposed to be protecting her and to do that you need to distance yourself from her, not look for her snuggled up against you in her bed.

Her bed!

He groaned so loudly he heard the noise echo back from the walls of her bedroom.

Damn it all.

He stood up and looked around then felt absurdly grateful when he saw his underpants lying on the floor.

Surely he'd be able to think better when he was at least partially clothed.

He'd barely pulled them on when there was a tap on the door and it opened far enough for Rowena to poke her head through the aperture.

'I heard a noise and thought you might be awake. Sarah's at the hospital. She checked on Margo during the night and has just gone back to see her before going to the surgery. Margo's actually heading into true labour now. I'm on my way to open up at the surgery. The storm's expected to last another day at least, possibly two. I spoke to Bart before the phones went out and he was going to put your animals in their pens last night and feed them, then check them again this morning. Bathroom's down the hall, there's hot water on the stove and plenty of food in the kitchen. Help yourself when you're ready.'

The head withdrew, and David, torn between fury that she'd managed to avoid even hinting at what had happened between them the previous evening and relief she had handled things so calmly, slumped back down on the bed and tried to figure out how he felt.

How he felt deep inside, in the cold heart of him which had been shut protectively away from personal closeness with a woman for a long, long time.

Frustrated was the easiest bit to figure. Given the way his body had reacted to even such a brief appearance, he was glad he'd found his underwear before she'd looked in.

Underwear! It was all very well to have retrieved this much, but where were the rest of his clothes? And what was happening about getting stuff from his house? Had Barry been serious when he'd said it was off-limits?

Man! He had to get with it here! Get his mind into gear.

Get some clothes first! Then reassess the strategy for protecting Rowena.

Mary-Ellen was stalking the island like a hungry lioness. If she were to get Rowena in her sights...

CHAPTER SEVEN

SARAH finished her examination of Margo, assured the now tired but still excitable young woman she was doing well then drew Barry outside.

'It's just a shame she came in so early,' she told the exhausted policeman. 'Both of you could easily have spent the night at home in bed. As I explained last night, those early contractions can go on for days.'

'But she's having real contractions now?' Barry asked. 'Things have started to happen, haven't they?'

Sarah smiled encouragingly at him, though she wondered just how much anxiety he could take. The fun part had barely started.

'Yes, they have, but she's still only at the early stages of true labour, what we call the latent phase. It will still be hours before things get interesting.'

'I don't know that I can take it,' he muttered.

'Then go home and get some sleep. Come back when you're rested, or when someone calls you.'

'But Margo has to be here, doesn't she? And if I'm not with her then I'm letting her down, aren't I?'

I should have knocked their heads together and sent them both home last night, Sarah thought—but last night Margo had been David's patient. He'd admitted her and up till eight-thirty had been the one checking on her.

Thinking of David reminded her.

'Barry, on another subject altogether, all my clothes are out at David's place. I can wear the same clothes for two days, but after that I'll probably get a bit ripe. I've patients to see this morning, but have you any objections to me going out there at lunchtime to get my suitcase? Or do you want the house as well as the shed sealed off?'

He ran his hands distractedly through his hair.

'I've been trying to think what to do! I've put a couple of fellows—fishermen who don't work at this time of year—out there to keep an eye on the house and sheds, but, honestly, what clues would anyone find after all this time?'

He paused and Sarah could see him thinking, then he glanced at his watch.

'Look, none of your patients will be early in weather like this—in fact, half won't turn up at all. Islanders tend to stay indoors when it storms. We've one police vehicle having a service today and Nick's got the other, but if you don't mind driving me out there now, you can get your belongings and pack some stuff for David as well. I'm only covering my back by not letting him out there, you know.'

Sarah started to say she didn't have a car, having left Rowena's for her to use and made the dash across the road on foot. Then she remembered David's—parked out the back of the hospital beside the small outbuilding.

She patted her pockets but found no keys.

'Heavens! I think I must have left the keys in it. Island mentality is getting to me.'

'Have you got a raincoat?' Barry asked, and Sarah nodded, then headed out on to the front veranda where she'd discarded the weatherproof coat and hat Rowena had found for her the previous evening.

She met up with Barry again at the back door and together they shrugged into the heavy oilskins designed to withstand the kind of rain the island could produce. Sarah added the sou'wester, pulling it down low over her forehead, while Barry produced a thick black beanie, which he rammed down over his curly hair.

Though the walkway between the buildings was covered by a curved tin roof, the rain, blown almost horizontal by the wind, still lashed beneath it.

'Are you ready to make the dash?' Barry asked.

'I guess,' Sarah said. 'Let's go!'

They hurried across the walkway then left its dubious shelter, Sarah heading for the driver's side of the car, Barry for the passenger's.

I should have let him drive in this weather, Sarah thought, but as she opened the door and at the same time heard Barry's alarmed oath, she was thankful she hadn't suggested it.

The body of the tall detective tumbled unceremoniously out of the vehicle, knocking Barry into the mud and landing right on top of him.

Muttering some swear words of her own, Sarah sloshed as fast as she could to Barry's aid. Her hands shaking with shock, she helped him up, then the pair of them stood and looked incredulously down at the man.

Almost automatically, Sarah knelt to feel for a pulse, but his pallor and stiffness, his blank-eyed stare, had already told them he was beyond medical assistance.

'I can't believe it,' she muttered, willing her mind to make the connection between sight and understanding.

Barry was looking equally bewildered, but he recovered first, his professional training coming to the fore.

'Do you think there's any chance you and I can get him into the outbuilding?' he asked. He was obviously worried about someone seeing the body, casting a glance towards the main hospital building as he spoke, but no one had ventured outside in this weather.

'I guess we could try,' Sarah said, knowing why Barry wanted it done this way. The less people who knew the better at this stage. 'Do you have the keys?'

His turn to feel in his pockets, though he met with more success than Sarah had earlier. He produced two keys—one for the padlock, the other for the door.

'Felt it was better to keep them on me,' he explained. 'I'll open up then we'll give moving him a go. If we can't do it I'll get Nick, but the longer we leave him here the more chance there'll be of someone seeing him. Then, as well as a storm, we'll have wholesale panic!'

Sarah looked at the dead man and considered the situation more rationally.

'I think we should get Nick anyway,' she said. 'You and I would have to drag him and that's not going to do much good to any trace evidence there might be. Among the things Jane brought over were some more plastic sheets. I'll cover him with one, then if we shift the body bag off the dissecting table in there—it's wheeled—we can bring it out here so all we have to do is lift him onto it.'

'Good idea. I'm glad someone's thinking straight in this place,' Barry told her. He unlocked the door, flipped a light switch and illuminated the depressing scene. 'Great! There's a phone extension. I'll call Nick from here.'

Sarah started to say that the lines were out, but as Barry was already dialling she realised he must have heard a tone so the break had evidently been mended.

She found the plastic sheet and hurried back outside, unfolding it with difficulty then realising she had nothing to weigh it down with once she spread it over him.

But keeping him dry seemed important—if irrational—so she pushed it over him and tucked it under his feet as if it were a blanket, then drew it up over his head, pushing it in under his body and holding the top part down with her hand.

It still flapped eerily in the gusting wind, and water dropped relentlessly from the brim of her hat onto the shiny white surface.

Beneath the plastic, she could feel the body—already cold.

Too cold for her to tell time of death?

Once again, she doubted whether she'd be called on to do an autopsy, but preliminary findings like time of death could help Barry seek out the…perpetrator or murderer?

Murderer, she decided, fear cramping her lungs as she imagined someone killing the policeman in her life.

As to cause of death? While the man was toppling out in a weird slow-motion kind of action, she'd seen the hole, like a ragged tear, just above his right temple. She'd seen pictures of the star-shaped wounds in books and knew it suggested he'd been shot at point-blank range, though how an ex-policeman had let someone hold a gun to his head, she couldn't understand.

Barry came to stand behind her, then she heard a vehicle approaching and the big police four-wheel drive churned mud beneath its wheels as it trundled up towards the building for the second time in two days.

Nick, his agility hampered by *his* wet weather gear, clambered out and came towards them.

'Inside first,' Barry told him, hustling the young policeman indoors.

They returned with the stainless-steel operating table, wheeling it close then standing beside Sarah to study the situation.

'It won't collapse like the new ones will, so I'll take the head end if you and Sarah can lift his legs,' Barry suggested. 'Are you sure you can manage, Sarah? I could get a wardsman to help.'

'Let's try it ourselves,' Sarah said, her agitation growing as concern for the man faded and questions of who and why now ran rampant in her mind.

Together they lifted the man, the plastic covering taking flight and flapping through the rain like a demented ghost.

'Up a little more!' Barry encouraged, and with a final heave they got him on the table.

'He's b-been shot!' Nick stuttered, his face pale as he surveyed his second corpse in as many days.

'I suppose we should have covered the head wound before we lifted him,' Sarah murmured. 'I guess we've made a mess of any evidence.'

'I already did that when I opened the door and he tumbled out. What were we supposed to do? Put him back in when who knows what he'd have picked up on the ground?'

'No. We've done the right thing,' Sarah assured Barry, but she shivered as the full import of the man's death struck home.

Still in the wet rain gear, she shoved her hands into the pockets to try to stop them shaking.

The fingers of her right hand struck a cold, hard object. She'd felt something bang against her legs as she'd run across the road earlier but hadn't wanted to investigate someone else's pockets.

Now the shape of the object added to her chills. She drew it out and held it on the palm of her hand, showing it, blue-black and deadly, to Barry.

'What the hell is *that*!'

Sarah knew it was a rhetorical question, and Barry was already searching for a glove and an evidence bag, but Nick took it literally.

'It's a gun. The man's been shot. Did you shoot him, Sarah?'

Sarah felt a surge of laughter, which she suspected might be hysterical, welling up inside her.

She let a small chuckle escape.

'No, I didn't, Nick, but as a policeman I'm sure you won't take my word for it. We're both strangers to the island. I might have known him on the mainland. He might have been my lover, and he jilted me!'

Nick studied her as if he might be able to see her guilt, and she regretted her silly suggestion.

Using gloved fingertips and picking it up by the barrel, Barry removed the gun from her hand and dropped it into a paper bag.

'You shouldn't joke about things like that,' Nick told her, and Sarah smiled at him.

'I know I shouldn't,' she assured him. 'But anything's possible, which is why you police always look at all angles of any case, not just at the obvious. I know darned well you'll check out the gun's registration, and not just accept my word it isn't mine.'

She turned to Barry.

'I'm assuming you don't want an autopsy, but what about time of death? Do you want an estimate?'

He nodded at her, his face grey with tiredness and pinched with worry. With automatic preciseness he patted down the man's pockets, retrieving a wallet from inside the jacket and a notebook and pen, a bit of twine and a near-empty packet of chewing gum from an outer pocket.

He tucked them into an evidence bag but it was obvious his mind was elsewhere.

'I should go and see Margo. I can't have a baby and these murders happening at the same time! And I'll have to notify people, homicide on the mainland, his family, do all of that.'

'Give Nick the keys and let him stay here while you go to your wife. As for notifying people, Paul Page isn't going to be any less dead in an hour or two—leave it until then. Could you ask Jane for a rectal thermometer, and get her to bring it out herself? It's only fair she should know she's got another body in her hospital.'

Barry nodded, then he said, 'Have you seen the gun before? Do you know who owns it?'

Sarah shook her head.

'It's not even my raincoat. Rowena lent it to me last night—she put it in the car. But the car was parked at the hospital, in the undercover area, on two separate occasions while I was in with Margo. The coat was in it but I didn't need it until this morning, when I walked across to the hospital and left Rowena's car for her to take to work.'

She considered her movements.

'I left the coat on the front veranda this morning. I guess

anyone could have slipped something into the pocket either during the night or while it hung on the peg out there.'

Sarah was shrugging out of the raincoat and Barry took it from her.

'Whose coat is it?'

'I don't know,' she said. 'I think it would be too big for Rowena. Perhaps it was her husband Peter's.'

But Barry was already looking inside the coat. Given the uniformity of effective rainwear, most people put their names or some other identifying mark on the flap beneath the collar.

'"David Wright"!' Barry read out loud, and Sarah felt her face grow hot although her body was suddenly very cold and shivery.

'David spent the night at Rowena's house—we both stayed there.'

She knew, as soon as she'd spoken, that it would have been better to keep her mouth shut, but the urge to defend her friend had overridden common sense.

'All night? He didn't leave the house? You can guarantee that?'

Barry might be tired but his policeman's instincts weren't dulled.

'No,' Sarah admitted, 'but he'd have to be a daft criminal to kill someone then hide the gun in his own raincoat pocket.'

'Or smart enough to think we'd think that!' Barry countered.

'A double bluff! I've read about those!' Nick said, so obviously intrigued by the 'story' element of the case he'd momentarily forgotten it was real—and someone was dead.

'I'll send Jane out,' Barry said, ignoring Nick's comment. He passed over the keys of the outbuilding to his colleague and walked away, his tall, solid figure made bulky yet somehow diminished by the muddy rain gear, his head bowed, no doubt contemplating the tasks ahead of him.

Not to mention the imminent arrival of his first child.

Jane appeared not long afterwards.

'This *is* fun!' she said gloomily. 'I've been here ten years and never had a murder. Now you've got—'

'Two in two days!' Nick finished for her.

His excitement was so obvious Sarah wanted to hit him, but hitting a policeman probably wasn't a good idea so she took the thermometer from Jane, thanked her and set it down while she once again donned gown, apron and gloves.

'I never did get you those wellies,' Jane said. 'Storm coming up and the hardware shop had sold out. Sorry about that.'

'It's OK, I'm not autopsying him.' Sarah told her, then, as Jane left the room, she began a superficial examination.

'Damn! I took the tape-recorder over to Rowena's to write up my notes from yesterday. Can you take notes if I dictate to you?'

Nick nodded and pulled out his notebook.

'Date and time first, as you do when you're taking your own notes,' Sarah told him. 'Then put this. "Lividity in the buttocks and underside of thighs, also the feet, suggest the deceased was killed where he sat and hadn't been moved prior to his falling out of the vehicle."'

'He fell out? How?' Nick asked.

'I'll explain later,' Sarah told him. 'Have you got all that?'

'Not quite,' the young man muttered. 'How do you spell the word you used?'

'Lividity?'

'That's the one.'

Sarah spelled it out for him, also explaining what it meant as she couldn't expect such a young policeman to have had much experience of forensic work. She repeated the rest of the opening sentence.

'The stiffness of the body suggests rigor is complete or almost complete,' she added, thinking it might be days before the body could be transported off the island, by which time the classic stiffening could have passed completely.

'Now I'm going to take a rectal temperature which means I'll have to remove some clothes—'

'Do I have to write this down?' Nick asked.

'No, not word for word everything I say, but we need records before we take off clothes. I know your camera was wrecked yesterday, but what about the Polaroid? Do you have more film for it? Or another camera we can use?'

Nick appeared to be considering this request, frowning as though mentally checking some office stock cupboard.

'I'm pretty sure there's more film in the office,' he said at last. 'I'll go and see.'

'No! You'd better not do that—not leaving me here with the body, especially after our visitor yesterday afternoon. They should have a camera at the hospital—I'll pop over there. You know not to touch anything, don't you?'

He nodded, though the defensive gleam in his eyes told her he had every intention of taking a better look at the body the moment she left the building.

He's only young, she reminded herself as she dashed through the wind-swept rain to the main building.

Where she found Barry, Rowena and David clustered on the back veranda, the tense looks on all three faces indicating that an argument was in progress.

Rowena claimed her support first.

'*You* tell him, Sarah! Tell him I spent the night with David. David's got some misguided sense of loyalty or chivalry or something and is denying it!'

David saw Sarah's surprise, but before he could forestall her reply she'd turned to Barry.

'I hope this isn't official—that you're not taking statements from these people with both of them together and no one taking notes.'

She then rounded on David and Rowena.

'And shouldn't you two be at the surgery, tending patients, rather than standing here arguing about chivalry? Go, off you go! Barry can see you later.'

'Margo wanted to see David so I drove him over,' Rowena explained to Sarah. 'The rain's keeping most of the patients at home.'

Sarah seemed satisfied, but David turned to Barry, wondering if he *had* been taking statements and what he'd made of Sarah's high-handed behaviour if he had. Then Rowena touched his arm, sending a shiver of memory flashing along his nerves.

But there were two bodies now—and though he had no proof Mary-Ellen was responsible for the detective's death, and absolutely no clue as to why she'd have killed her sister—if indeed she had—it was more important than ever to distance himself from Rowena.

A mishmash of dread and suspicion flashed through his mind so quickly that little time elapsed between her touch and his reaction, which was to step away—again—and then deliberately turn to Barry.

'I take it my car as well as my house and property is now off-limits.'

When Barry nodded affirmation of this, David ducked his head down deeper into the collar of the borrowed coat and said to Rowena, 'I'm going to dash through the rain, rather than drive back.'

He saw her flinch away from his coldness, and told himself it was good. The sooner she got the message the better.

But she hadn't got it at all, he realised later when, alone in the little building, he tackled her about her lie.

She'd come into the consulting room to tell him Mr O'Brien hadn't turned up, and the almost overwhelming urge to take her in his arms and kiss the breath out of her shocked him into harshness. Gripping the edge of his desk to keep his hands from temptation, he glared at the cause of this new complication.

'What on earth made you tell Barry we'd spent the night together?'

She stepped forward, though cautiously, as if she'd correctly read his anger.

'The body was found in your car, and a gun in your raincoat pocket. I knew you hadn't gone out. I'm a light sleeper and I'd have heard you, but I didn't think Barry would believe me.'

'And you think he'd believe you spent the night with me?' David demanded, though it was a battle to maintain his rage with memories of lamplight from the hall flickering across her bare skin getting in the way.

'Not if you keep flinching away every time I touch you!' Rowena retorted. 'Do I repulse you so much? Is your mind still so tangled up in your love for your dead wife you can't bear to have another woman close?'

The passion in the questions startled him, then he realised the words were filled with pain. With all his being he wanted to go to her, to hold her and comfort her—tell her how he felt.

But he'd seen Rowena happy—after the kiss in the bedroom, before he'd slapped her down that time! And she glowed with it! Her eyes shone, and her skin took on a lustre like the sheen of expensive pearls. There was no way it could be hidden.

Don't even think about it, his mind warned his heart. Hurt her if you have to—if it will keep her from far worse harm. The kind of harm he instinctively believed Mary-Ellen could do!

Then, because he couldn't look her in the eye while he told a lie, he picked up some papers from his desk and fiddled with them.

'I suppose that's it,' he said, hoping his voice wouldn't

crack as he betrayed the love she'd given so freely—the pleasure they'd shared. 'You'll just have to put last night's behaviour down to shock and frustration, I guess. It's been a long time for me, and you were there.'

You were there! The phrase rang like a carillon in Rowena's head, though the bells must have been out of tune for the noise was discordant enough to hurt her ears.

'Glad I could be of service!' she muttered at him, then remembered another meaning of the word and snapped, 'Literally, I guess,' before charging out of the room and slamming the door, hard, behind her.

Back at the reception desk she huddled on her chair, folding her arms around her body in an effort to warm herself. But the coldness was deep inside her and no amount of arm-rubbing was going to help, any more than a tablet would have eased the pain.

The ringing of the phone startled her so much she stared at it for a moment, uncertain what to do.

Maybe longer than a moment, for David appeared in his doorway, perhaps thinking she'd left the building and he'd have to answer it himself.

'I thought the lines were down,' she muttered as she picked it up.

Nick Walters introduced himself, then said, 'I don't suppose you could give the doctor here—the lady doctor, Sarah—a hand again. I'm taking photos and taking notes, but she needs help to put things into bags and label them. Barry's with Margo and Jane's busy with both of them and Jane says the aides shouldn't have to do it.'

Rowena could hear frustration in his voice.

She glanced up to where David still stood, grim-faced and pale, in the doorway.

'Can you manage here without me?'

He looked around the empty waiting room and gave a mocking laugh.

'Probably for ever if this is how the islanders are going to react to hearing their doctor's a murder suspect.'

'It's the weather, not the murder!' Rowena retorted. 'And stop feeling sorry for yourself. Do something positive. Get the paperwork you were going to dump on Sarah done.'

She heard a squawking noise and realised she was still holding the receiver. In fact, she'd been waving it at David as she spoke. Now she lifted it to her ear again and promised Nick she'd be right over.

'I should start charging them for my labour,' she grumbled at David as she left, because grumbling at him was better than bursting into tears every time she considered what he'd said.

She took her car but couldn't drive close to the outbuilding as a barricade had been erected to stop all entry.

'We've got crime-scene tape but Barry said it would only worry people if we put it up so I used the plastic barriers we keep to close the main street for the New Year party,' Nick explained as she dashed through the rain and burst into the building.

'Why on earth do you want to stop cars driving in?' Rowena asked him. 'You don't seriously think you're going to find tyre prints out there after all this rain? Especially when your police vehicle has already driven in.'

'That's what Barry said,' Nick complained, 'but it's correct procedure.'

'Seems to me he's been up all night reading the procedures manual,' Sarah teased. 'Probably shot the guy to get a bit of practice at following an investigation.'

Nick's protest was swallowed up by the noise of rain and wind as the door opened.

All three of them turned towards it, but no one came in. Rowena, having just removed her rain gear, was the closest and she hurried to shut it again.

'I couldn't have shut it properly,' she said, and apologised to the others, although she was the one who'd been wet by the gust.

'Slip the lock across as well,' Sarah suggested. 'With the force of the wind it could blow open again.'

The words made sense but it was the tightness in them that scared Rowena. If someone as sensible as Sarah was freaked out by the goings-on, things must be serious.

Of course they're serious, she scolded herself as she draped a gown over her clothes then added a plastic apron and picked up a pair of gloves. You've been so hung up over your feelings for David, you're ignoring the fact there's a murderer on the island.

Somehow 'perpetrator' no longer seemed strong enough.

'I'm going to cut off his trousers. Because he's stiffened in such an awkward position, I'll need help to get the bits off,' Sarah explained. 'Then I want them bagged and labelled.'

She picked up a large pair of shears and began by slicing through the man's belt at the back.

'Wouldn't it be easier to undo it?' Rowena asked.

'Not when the most likely fingerprints would be around the buckle,' Nick told her..

'But they'd be his—that's all,' Rowena pointed out.

'Probably,' Nick said, 'but what if someone else dressed him?'

'Oh!'

'I wonder why he wasn't wearing a raincoat—or some kind of protection?' Nick asked, and Sarah stared at him as if he'd grown another head.

'You're right! I didn't even think of that. And he's not wet, his clothes aren't even damp, yet it's been raining since we came out of this building last night. He came out with us—surely he didn't get in the car then. I'm pretty sure we'd have noticed if he had.'

'So another car must have driven up there,' Nick said,

with the smug smile of someone who'd just been proved correct.

'Doesn't mean there'd be any tyre tracks left,' Rowena retorted.

Sarah held up her hand.

'Peace, my children!'

However, Rowena wasn't worried about arguing with Nick—she'd had a brilliant notion.

'But the car was there all along. So David couldn't have driven the man up there! And there was no second car in the drive this morning so someone else has to be involved, driving him through the rain and leaving him there.'

She offered it triumphantly as Sarah asked her to bag the cut belt and ruined segment of trousers exactly as they were.

'But David could have arranged for the chap to meet him—say at the hospital—then suggested they sit in the car to have a talk,' Nick suggested.

Rowena glared at him.

'Trust you to think of an objection!' she muttered, folding the cloth carefully then ruining the effect by jamming it angrily into the bag. 'You sound as if you *want* it to be David, when you must know he's as gentle as a lamb and goes out of his way to *save* life. Look at the animals he tended during the bush fires.'

'Here,' Sarah interrupted. 'Give me a hand to lift him. In fact, Nick and I will do it, and you pull the material out from underneath him.'

'The material' was the other half of the man's trousers, now removed in one long piece.

'Pop it in a bag and label it,' Sarah told Rowena. 'And note the time again for me, Nick. I'm going to take his body temperature then see if we can work out when it happened.'

Rowena was relieved to have her attention recalled to

work. She probably wasn't doing David's cause much good by defending him so vehemently.

Especially as he'd made it obvious he had no desire for her support.

None at all!

'It's 35.8 degrees Celsius. He's a big man so he'd cool more slowly than a thin person— No, don't write the comment down, Nick, just the temperature. I'm only thinking aloud. It's always easier to work in Fahrenheit because a body in a room at sixty degrees cools at one and a half degrees an hour, but in Celsius the scale uses a three-hour graph.'

'Do you have any idea what she's talking about?' Rowena asked Nick.

He grinned at her, the antagonism between them forgotten in their mutual interest in the science.

'Some,' he admitted, while Sarah, with a pen and paper, muttered to herself as she scribbled graph lines and figures. 'Say he started off with a normal temperature of just over 37 degrees Celsius. Then, as his body cools, this temperature drops. Scientists have worked out how much it cools an hour and now that she knows it's gone down just over one degree, Sarah's working out how many hours ago he died.'

'But she was talking about a room at sixty degrees Fahrenheit,' Rowena reminded him. 'And she's read the thermometer in Celsius.'

'Sixty degrees Fahrenheit is about fifteen and half degrees Celsius,' Sarah said over her shoulder. 'That any help? No, it wouldn't be, because he wasn't in a room, he was in a car, and the car was out in the open...'

She turned around now.

'Would you know what the temperature was last night?'

'Ten degrees Celsius,' Nick said promptly.

'He does the weather reports for the island,' Rowena explained to the surprised doctor.

'Damn!' Sarah muttered. 'I know lividity and rigor aren't reliable, but it doesn't make sense.'

''What doesn't?''

Rowena and Nick spoke together.

'Thirty-five point eight degrees in the cold with a man his size would give me about six hours since the time of death, possibly less, putting it at what? One to two-thirty in the morning?'

'So wouldn't that be a perfect time to kill someone?' Rowena asked.

Sarah sighed.

'It destroys the ''meeting someone'' scenario. I mean, what person in his right mind, particularly an ex-policeman, would agree to meet someone they didn't know at such an hour? Especially someone you might possibly suspect of murder.'

'But remember he was a cop—and a big fellow. He'd have been confident he could handle it.'

Sarah turned to Nick and pointed her pen at him.

'You're young and enthusiastic now, but don't ever, ever think that just because you're a policeman you can handle things!' she told him. 'No! If you consider it logically, Nick, his training should have made him more wary, not less.'

'Forget his reaction for a moment,' Rowena interrupted. 'Apart from the unlikelihood of a meeting at that time, what else doesn't fit? You mentioned other things.'

Sarah grinned at her.

'Easily sidetracked, aren't we? The lividity is stable, which happens in about six to ten hours and can continue for up to twenty-four. Which means if he'd been shifted after it sets, the discoloration would remain where it is now. But as a way of estimating time of death, it's not much use except that we know it's at least six hours since he died, but I'd say, for a man his size and the extent of discoloration, it would be longer than that. See how the skin remains red when I press against it. Earlier than that, it would blanch—go white—when I pressed it.'

'What about the cold?' Nick asked, but Sarah shook her head.

'Lividity isn't affected by temperature, but the rigor is. The cold should have slowed the process but the body has the stiffness of someone who's been dead twelve hours or longer. I guess we might have more idea when it starts to wear off, although that could be thirty to thirty-six hours later so it's not accurate either.'

'So what am I writing down?' Nick asked.

'Just the body temperature and the outdoor temperature last night,' Sarah told him. 'Let the scientists on the mainland work it out. Actually, they have a new way of measuring the time of death, using factors involved in the release of potassium from the blood as it breaks down, so they should be able to come up with a more accurate estimate.'

'If we ever get him over to the mainland,' Nick said. 'The way the weather looks, it could be days before a plane can land. In the meantime, he'll have to go on ice.'

'Which could alter things considerably,' Sarah said, frowning at the dead man as if he were personally responsible for the problem.

Rowena understood her dilemma because her own frustration at a lack of a definite time was gnawing at her stomach. She and Sarah had been up and moving around the house until after ten, then Sarah had gone over to the hospital at ten-thirty and again at two-thirty.

The last time rang a bell. She turned to Sarah.

'Two-thirty? You were out at that time. You didn't see anyone?'

CHAPTER EIGHT

'LURKING out the back?' Sarah thought for a moment. 'I didn't even look. It was raining and blowing hard enough to make visibility practically nil. I drove over, parked under cover, went in through the side entrance to the hospital and came back out the same way. Though a hospital is a strange choice of a site to kill someone, given that it's the one place in any town where people are not only on duty all night but are actively moving around.'

'But last night, any moving around would have been internal,' Rowena said. 'Not even the most die-hard of smokers would have ventured onto the veranda in the wind.'

'It still seems risky,' Sarah said, frowning at the man again. 'And I don't like two-thirty. I know body temperature is the most reliable of three unreliable factors, but the other signs should at least relate to it.'

'Perhaps when we get witnesses, people who've seen him around, we'll be able to narrow it down a bit,' Nick suggested.

'Seen him around where?' Rowena snapped at him. 'Drinking at the pub until closing time, which last night, given the weather, was probably eight-thirty. Or taking in the sights of the town of Winship—on a night when a gale's blowing, the power and phones are off and the heavens have opened?'

'Someone will have seen him,' Nick said stubbornly. 'The woman he's with, for a start. And the folk wherever he's staying. He's at the motel, isn't he?'

'I don't know and I don't care,' Rowena said, then she turned to Sarah. 'Do you need me for anything else?'

The surprise in Sarah's eyes told Rowena she probably

sounded as demented as she felt, but she needed to get out—away from the body they were discussing so heartlessly—away from death.

Why the panic? she asked herself when Sarah had thanked her for her help and she was struggling into her raincoat, outside the room instead of inside.

'Because it's real, not just a game!'

She said the words aloud—said them slowly as if they had to be chewed over before they'd come out.

And no mater where the speculation went—with times of death and possible scenarios for how the man had come to be in David's car—David would remain the focus of attention. And would remain in danger.

She pressed her hand against her chest and looked fearfully towards his car.

Why?

Wasn't that the question?

Why was all this happening?

Forget about Paul Page for the moment. She was fairly certain his had been a follow-up kind of death. Consider Sue-Ellen. Why would someone kill David's wife?

Rowena buttoned up her coat and felt in the pocket for a rain-hat, but remembered she'd lent hers to Sarah.

'Bad luck!' she muttered to herself. 'So your hair will get wet—so what?'

After a final look at the car, she turned towards the surgery and flung herself into the rain, dashing down the drive, around the barriers and across the deserted street.

She left her dripping outer clothes in the porch, absently noting Peter's old slicker hanging on a peg.

But nothing else—no customers today.

She hurried inside and, after a perfunctory knock, opened the consulting-room door.

'Why would someone want to kill your wife?' she demanded.

David looked up and her foolish heart imagined she'd

caught a glow of pleasure in his eyes before he quenched it with a scowl and said, 'I presume you have a reason for asking your question.'

'Oh, stop being so stuffy!' she told him, coming in and flopping into the chair across the desk from him. 'OK, so you don't want me as a lover, but we're still friends so let's figure this out. It *has* to go back to her. This man's death can't be totally unrelated, but we don't know anything about him so we have to start with Sue-Ellen.'

There! She'd said it! Said the name of the woman.

David shook his head.

'Do you think I haven't tried to work that out?'

'Money!' Rowena suggested. 'They were a wealthy family—the parents were dead. Did she inherit much—have a lot of money of her own?'

Then, as she realised where this question was headed, she said, 'Oh!' in a weak voice and slumped into a chair.

'Exactly!' David said. 'Why do you think I was chief suspect? Only she didn't have a lot of money. The family had an expensive lifestyle, so there wasn't a huge fortune left. Sue-Ellen inherited enough which, if properly invested, would have given her a nice bit of extra income for the rest of her life but she was brought up to have the best and have it now. Instant gratification.'

'Nothing left?'

The question brought a grim smile.

'Nothing,' David confirmed. 'We know that for sure because the police had some notion I'd taken the money and secreted it away so, on legal advice, every purchase Sue had made, everything she'd spent over the years immediately preceding her death, was investigated. I insisted the lawyers go through every credit-card bill, every store account. She'd spent it all right!'

'But that's wonderful,' Rowena told him. 'It removes your motive for killing her.'

'Only if I could prove I'd known it was all gone!'

This time the smile was slightly more relaxed and, though she knew she shouldn't, Rowena found herself responding to it.

She smiled back.

David looked at her. The neat knot of hair was damp and dishevelled so little ribbons of hair now curled wetly around her face, framing the oval shape in the way ringlets framed the faces of women in sketches of Regency times.

The grey eyes, so steadfast, were still wary, but they'd lost their look of hurt—which he'd inflicted.

Would pointing out the obvious inflict more?

'It only removed one motive,' he reminded her. 'Spouses murder each other every day of the week, and only rarely is money involved.'

He watched Rowena nod and realised she was listing other motives to herself—passion and jealousy sprang immediately to most people's minds, and Rowena wasn't to know these were two emotions he'd gone beyond in his relationship with Sue-Ellen.

Nor could he tell her.

The doorbell announced a new arrival and saved him from further discussion. Though he was less interested in why his wife had been killed—to him it was totally unbelievable that someone would *want* to kill her—than in where the trunk had been when the police had searched his farm four years ago. He knew the shed had been searched, and if it had been there at the time, the trunk would have been opened. So where had it come from? And when?

'Mrs Robinson's here about the result of her blood tests—I think they came through the other day.'

As Rowena ushered the woman in, David sorted through the patient files on his desk. With so many people not turning up—they'd probably only been coming to check out Sarah anyway—the files were out of order.

'Hello, Pat!' he greeted the older woman. 'How have you been?'

'Good!' she told him firmly, but he'd learned Pat Robinson wasn't one to complain.

In fact, the stoicism of the islanders, the women in particular, had been something he'd noticed early on. Perhaps their isolation made them less reliant on outside help, so they battled on regardless of the obstacles in their way.

Rowena was typical of the breed...

'No nausea from the drugs?'

'None,' Pat Robinson said firmly. Diverting his mind from Rowena to his patient, he thought again of stoicism and wondered if she'd tell him if she *was* feeling nauseous.

'The blood tests show no abnormality but, as I explained, they wouldn't reveal symptoms of Parkinson's, only rule out anything else.'

'So what would reveal I've got it?' Pat asked, and David grinned at her.

'Apart from my diagnosis? A CT scan—the CT stands for computerised tomography, which is a fancy name for taking images of a slice of your body. It enables us to see what changes may have taken place in your brain and is less bothersome than doing a lumbar puncture to check your cerebrospinal fluid to see the results of these changes.'

Pat nodded as if she understood but, then, most patients simply adapted what they knew of more familiar X-ray images, coupled it with the knowledge of what computers could do to alter pictures on their television sets and worked out their own concept of the end result.

'I'd have to go to the mainland,' Pat said in the tone of voice most people reserved for visits to the dentist.

'For further tests, yes.'

'But you think I've got it anyway,' she persisted.

'From the loss of movement in your face, and the rigidity in your neck—remember when I tried to raise your arm and turn it and the muscles in your shoulder were hard to move—yes, I think you have. That's why I started treatment with the levodopa.'

'It's helping me,' Pat assured him. 'I can walk better. I know I don't have the shakes like you think of with Parkinson's yet, but I was having trouble getting started when I stood up. And I can write better as well. It was hard to get my fingers working before.'

Maybe it was the mention of fingers, but as she spoke, David noticed the little movement of her fingers across her thumb, the pin-rolling movement typical of Parkinson's.

'There are exercises you can do, simple things to help slow the rate at which the disease progresses,' he told her, when they'd discussed the pros and cons of further testing and he'd accepted that she didn't want to go to the mainland.

'These are for the face muscles to keep them toned.' He demonstrated the eyebrow-raising and wrinkling of the forehead, went on to mouth-opening and -closing, cheek-puffing and whistling. 'I've a card with them on,' he told her, when they'd both stopped laughing at the foolish faces he'd been pulling. 'And stay active, though I doubt I have to tell *you* that. When walking, hold your hands behind your back—it will help straighten your neck and keep the tremors still.'

He was examining Pat as he talked, taking her blood pressure while standing, then asking her to lie down for a resting pressure.

'I'll take blood as well, to see how the drug's reacting in your bloodstream, and I want you in every week for the next six weeks to monitor the levels. After that we'll string the visits out more. The problem with the drug is that it can become less effective and we might have to use something else as well.'

'I'll be doped to my eyebrows,' Pat told him, but she offered her arm for the needle and waited patiently while he took a sample of her blood.

He then dropped eight paper-clips on the floor, a little test he'd initiated on her first visit.

She bent and picked them up, then placed them triumphantly on the desk. 'See, I did it!'

'Let's hope you can continue to do it,' David told her, knowing it was a sure way to tell when her condition was deteriorating and if a different drug regime would be needed.

The visit was over, and he'd reminded her to make an appointment with Rowena before leaving, when she said, 'That chap didn't go home to the motel last night. The one who's here with your sister-in-law.'

Though used to the way everyone knew everything on the island, David still shook his head in disbelief.

'And how do you know?'

'Because he left his light on in his motel room and it shines into my yard. Even with the rain, I could see the yellow square lit up on the peach trees out the back.'

'Maybe he's afraid of the dark and sleeps with the light on,' David suggested, while his stomach cramped with the knowledge of just where the man had been.

'And with curtains open? I don't think so,' Pat told him. 'Anyway, he wasn't there this morning when I went down early to check on the chooks. I could see right through the window and the bed hadn't been slept in.'

Was it curiosity disguised as concern, or simply the islanders' habit of watching out for each other? David wondered, but he didn't offer any further explanations or encourage any more gossip.

There'd be enough talk around shortly, without him adding to it.

As he showed Pat out, Rowena signalled to him so, when the older woman had departed, he walked across to the reception desk.

He could feel his heart stirring and his body stiffening, just looking at the woman, but steeled himself to hide these facts.

'Sarah phoned to say she'd check on Margo. Apparently

things are moving faster now, and Margo, now Nell's not here, has decided she'd rather have a woman deliver her baby.'

'Or her husband's decided he'd rather not have a murderer deliver his!'

Was it the strain of the pretence with Rowena that had prompted the bitter remark? Whatever it was, he knew it had shocked and possibly hurt her, for her face paled and the lines of strain around her mouth deepened.

But when she raised her eyes to his, it was anger he saw there, not pain.

'Oh, please!' she muttered at him. 'Let's not start that kind of nonsense. You know you didn't kill your wife or the detective, so get your act into gear and damn well prove it.'

She glared at him, then rather spoilt the effect by saying, 'Do you think I'm too old to learn to swear more effectively? Damn's about my limit, and it seems far too weak to handle what's been happening around here lately!'

He wanted to smile—and to touch her, hold her. To let her know she'd brightened up his day with her worries over the appropriateness of 'damn'—but two people were dead, and *someone* had killed them.

'You're right. I've got to quit whining and work out a solution. We've ruled out money, though if it had been Mary-Ellen who'd been killed it would be different. She went through three short-term husbands, each wealthier than the previous one and each leaving her with more accumulated funds!'

Rowena watched the way his brow furrowed just on one side when he frowned. He'd end up with a single frown mark instead of two. Her eyes feasted on him, feeding all the inner longings, reminding her of the pleasure they'd shared the previous evening.

Well, it had been a joy for her, and if it had been nothing more than easing physical frustration for David, it didn't really matter because she still had her memories of a passionate, fiery lover.

'What if it was a mistake?'

The question surprised her nearly as much as it surprised David, who was looking at her as if she were mad.

'Sorry! That came out of my subconscious, but the pair looked so alike. What if someone intended to kill Mary-Ellen, and killed Sue-Ellen by mistake?'

The furrow deepened.

'We come back to why.'

'An ex-husband unhappy over the settlement? Hadn't she just left number three? Perhaps he didn't want her to leave? If she had so many husbands, you'd suspect she probably had lovers as well. A jealous lover?'

'Those are all the reasons I was prime suspect,' David reminded her. 'Once they found Sue-Ellen's lover, and he claimed she was leaving me, it made the police case against me so much stronger.'

'We're not talking about you!' Rowena retorted. 'Concentrate on Mary-Ellen. Who'd get her money if she died?'

David shrugged, a tired movement of his shoulders which suggested that even thinking about it made him feel uncomfortable.

'Sue-Ellen, I suppose. Mary-Ellen had no children. I never asked. For all I know, she may be leaving it to charity and has always intended to do just that.'

Rowena thought about it.

'Well, we know it can't be that anyway, because neither of them could murder herself in mistake for her sister. They'd be the only two people in the world who always knew for sure who was who.'

David looked at her with such total bemusement she chuckled.

'I got caught up in my own cleverness there, didn't I?'

'You did indeed,' he said, and for a moment it seemed as if things might be getting back to normal between them.

Which was when Barry walked in.

'Sarah's with Margo—she's given her an epidural and I haven't much time. Have you still got the big cool-room out on the farm? The one the old fellow used to keep his seasonal fruit in?'

David nodded.

'But it hasn't been turned on for years. Why—?'

He stopped short and Rowena knew he'd figured it out. With the airport closed, and the seas too rough for small boats, the bodies couldn't leave the island until Monday at the earliest.

'Do you want me to go out and clean it out—see if it works?'

'If you wouldn't mind,' Barry told him. 'We could use the fish co-op—there's plenty of freezer space because it's off-season—but everything that goes in there comes out smelling of fish. And the fellow I spoke to at the hospital on the mainland suggested a cold-room was better than a freezer.'

'Definitely better as far as deterioration is concerned, but you're sure it won't affect the case, storing him on my property?'

Barry frowned at him.

'Of course it would if you went out on your own! Why didn't *I* think of that? We'll have to wait until the baby arrives, then I'll drive you out.'

'I can't believe this conversation!' Rowena told the two men. 'Only yesterday—no, the day before yesterday—everything was normal. Now you two are discussing the merits of freezers versus cold storage for bodies as if it's nothing out of the way.'

'Day before yesterday all *I* had to worry about was whether Junior was going to be a girl or a boy!' Barry reminded her. 'And if it was a girl, how I was going to survive her adolescence! Do you think I wanted to find dead bodies littered all over the island? Falling out on me when I open car doors?'

'Have you had any sleep at all?' David asked, reacting, as Rowena had, to the level of hysteria in Barry's voice.

The policeman rubbed his hands through his hair, scratching at his scalp as if to massage some sanity into his brain.

'Not much,' he admitted. 'But the moment Junior's here and I know Margo's OK, I'm going home to catch a bit of a kip.'

He looked directly at David.

'After which, I'll have a second murder to investigate, won't I?'

The words sent sharp tendrils of fear into the soft parts of Rowena's body, but she said nothing, though she did watch Barry as he walked to the door, and sighed with relief when he finally departed.

David heard the sigh and ached to comfort her, but that way lay danger. Rowena was right in that Mary-Ellen wouldn't have murdered her sister by mistake, but he felt, instinctively, the danger all centred around his sister-in-law. She'd been on the island when Sue-Ellen had disappeared, though whether his wife had died then—indeed, whether she'd died here—remained to be seen. All he knew was that by the time he arrived to join her for a holiday, she was gone.

But now Mary-Ellen was back—and a second person was dead. Fear, not for himself but for Rowena, clutched at his intestines.

'I don't want you mixed up in this,' he said to her, 'I don't want you talking about it, or trying to solve it, or in any way getting involved.'

'And you can stop me?' she challenged him, her chin tilting upward and her eyes glinting with the light of battle.

'I can *ask* you to keep out of it. Even beg you, Rowena.

It's dangerous to meddle in police matters, and foolish. You never know where the meddling may lead.'

'I have no intention of meddling in police matters,' she told him huffily, then, because she knew he'd read the lie in her eyes, she dropped her gaze back down to the papers on her desk.

Now that he was unobserved, he could look at her, see her anew as he remembered the woman who'd met and matched his passion the previous evening, giving and taking pleasure with an uninhibited enthusiasm which had escalated his own excitement.

So much so that even recollecting it had his body tightening with desire while his head roared the warnings he knew he dared not ignore.

He lifted the appointment book, pretending to study it while trying to work out why he'd taken so long to fall in love with her.

He knew the physical and mental reactions to what he'd gone through after Sue-Ellen's disappearance had been normal. Almost like a textbook case, he'd followed the trail of shock, apathy and despair. Waiting for the growth that should come out of all human experience to finally arrive.

'Spent a bloody sight too long at the apathy stage,' he muttered to himself.

'Something wrong? Someone booked in who shouldn't be?'

Rowena looked up from her work, her clear eyes repeating the question—or possibly asking other questions. Ones he couldn't—or wouldn't—answer.

'No, no!' he assured her, and wished he had something else to look at.

Because although he knew he had to put emotional distance between them, instinct told him to stay close to her. To protect her!

He dropped the book on the counter and walked back into the consulting room.

Protect her, indeed! She'd be better protected if he left the island—and that being impossible right now, if he went down to the far end to stay with Ted.

Now, that wasn't a bad idea, though first he had to go out to the farm with Barry and see if he could get the motor which chilled the cold room working.

He walked back out.

'I'm going over to the hospital to check on Margo. Phone me on the mobile if any patient happens to wander in.'

Rowena watched him go. After three years, she was closely enough attuned to him to know he had more on his mind than the murders, but what? The mood swings, quick anger and furrowed brow all suggested he was deeply worried about something. Panicky, almost, and David never panicked.

Not for an instant did she believe it could have anything to do with the murder of Mary-Ellen's tall investigator, but what else could it possibly be?

'The baby finally arrived—a girl they're calling Ruby, bless her little heart.'

Sarah burst through the door with the energy that came from a release of tension. 'Thank heavens!' she added. 'I'd have committed murder myself if it had gone on much longer, only I'm not sure which one I'd have killed—the mother or the father.'

'It's their first,' Rowena said, offering an excuse for the couple.

'And last as far as I'm concerned. If David ever asks me to hold the fort again, I'll check she's not pregnant before I agree.'

She spoke so naturally, assuming David would still be here in the future, Rowena felt relieved. Though not relieved enough to drop the subject.

'Do you remember what time it was when Mary-Ellen

and the detective came into the outbuilding yesterday afternoon?'

Sarah frowned at her.

'I'd forgotten they were there. It was late, not long before we finished. Which was, what?'

'About seven,' Rowena reminded her.

'Then I'd say they were there at six.'

'And David's car was there and the keys were in it. Right beside the building.'

'Yes, but that's far too early for the man to have been killed. And too risky at that time with people moving about, visitors and staff pottering around. Sure, it was raining but, no, I can't see it happening then, either practically or from the state of the body.'

'No, but it means they knew the car was there. What if Mary-Ellen saw it, then suggested they come back later and have a look for clues? He'd have gone to the car with her, whereas it's unlikely he'd have arranged to meet anyone he didn't know in someone else's car.'

'Unless David arranged it,' Sarah said, 'which is exactly what the police will think because they always look at the obvious first. The more obscure suspicions, and the positively bizarre ideas, come a little further down the investigative track.'

She hesitated for a moment, then said, 'Leaving David out, your scenario of Mary-Ellen suggesting they have a look is feasible—as long as no one asks for what—but why would Mary-Ellen kill him? She brought him over here, presumably to investigate. They'd been here, what, two days? Why bump him off now?'

'I don't know,' Rowena said crossly. 'I'm just saying he'd have gone to the car with her and sat beside her without considering for an instant he might come to any harm. He couldn't have been too suspicious of whoever it was to have just sat there and let someone shoot him.'

'And policemen are by nature and training very suspicious,' Sarah said, obviously coming around to Rowena's way of thinking.

'But motive remains a problem. Why bring the man over here then kill him?'

'To implicate David?' Rowena suggested, then she shivered. 'Though that would mean premeditation. Something she'd cold-bloodedly planned. I can't believe anyone would do such a thing! Would hate someone so much they'd kill another person to get their revenge.'

'No, revenge as a motive for murder seems very weak, unless there's a history of such behaviour in your family. Money always seems far more likely to me,' Sarah said. 'Or to protect a secret—that's done often enough.'

She spoke as if she'd had experience of it, or maybe she was just tired.

'You've had a rough welcome to Three Ships, haven't you?' Rowena said. 'Anyway, we've no customers. Everyone who was booked has cancelled because of the weather, so let's leave a sign on the door and go to an early lunch.'

But as she wrote the note, her mind still played with motives. Money? Unless Mary-Ellen was married to the detective, that wouldn't work. But what if he'd discovered something?

'It's ridiculous!' she told Sarah when they'd dashed along the wind-swept street to the café and were once again shedding their bulky rainwear in the sheltered area outside the door. 'Mary Ellen's the logical suspect as far as killing the man's concerned, but if she had secrets to hide, why bring him here? Why take the risk he'd find out something? It doesn't make sense.'

'So what's new?' Sarah responded. 'Up to now, none of it has. Sue-Ellen's body found in a trunk on a property which was searched when she disappeared. Tell me that makes sense! The indicators of the time of the man's death…'

They pushed into the interior of the café, where overheated air hit them like the blast from a furnace.

'Indicators of the time of death!'

Sarah grabbed Rowena's arm.

'I've been assuming the car was cold—the same temperature as outside—but if he and someone had got into the car to talk, wouldn't they have turned on the heater? We've got to find Barry.'

Rowena began to explain he'd intended going out to David's property as soon as the baby arrived, but Sarah was already out the door, dragging her damp coat back on.

'Nick will do—I just need someone to check the car.'

'Surely someone's done that!' Rowena protested, but as Sarah obviously wasn't going to be stopped, she pulled her own coat on as well. Fortunately the rain had eased, though the wind persisted, flinging damp scuds across the street every few minutes.

Nick was at the police station, entering notes into a computer.

'Yes, I checked the car, removed the keys and locked it so no one could get in.'

'Was the engine running—no, of course, it wouldn't have been, I'd have noticed.' Sarah answered her own question before Nick had a chance. 'Was the key in the "on" position? Or turned part-way so the auxiliary functions had power?'

Nick frowned at her.

'I had to turn it to take it out, so I guess it was on. Why? Are you worried you left the engine running?'

Of course she isn't, Rowena wanted to say as Sarah's line of questioning suddenly made sense. But saying something might remind Nick that, while Sarah had a legitimate right to the information, she didn't, and he might ask her to leave.

She tried to look as uninterested as possible, while Nick, who either loved camera work, or had no reliance on his memory, went through the photos he'd taken of the car's interior.

'You'd need a magnifying glass to see it clearly, but I've a good shot of the key in the ignition.'

'Good work,' Sarah said.

'The photos were for back-up and evidence.'

He looked up at Sarah as if he'd only just begun to wonder where the questions were leading.

'Why do you want to know?'

She studied him for a moment.

'If the heater was on in the car, it will have made a difference to both the body cooling and the rigor. If external heat affected the body temperature for a couple of hours, it would keep the body warmer, but would act as an accelerant to the rigor, though it wouldn't have any effect on the lividity.'

'It would also explain why his clothes were dry,' Nick muttered, 'even though he'd had to come through some degree of rain to get there. I've a photo of the dashboard.' Nick sorted excitedly through his snaps once again.

'Wouldn't it be easier to go across to the car and have a look?' Rowena couldn't keep out of things any longer. 'See where the temperature control is set rather than looking at photos.'

'We could do that,' Nick told her, 'but I don't see what the temperature control will prove. Day like yesterday, David would have had the heater on.'

'Actually, I was the last one who drove it, and I didn't have the heater on because the air coming out of it smelt musty to me,' Sarah told him. 'But if it was on, do you think if you knew how much fuel was in the tank you'd be able to work out how long the engine would have run before it stopped? Or would the battery have gone flat? I'm not much on car engines and their workings. It was certainly cold when Barry and I opened it this morning.'

'I suppose there's a way to work out something like that!' Nick said, his tone dubious, 'but the lab people would do it more accurately.'

Sarah was now sorting through the photos.

'I thought you took more photos of the trunk and the body when we were in the autopsy room,' Sarah said, spreading the photos on the desk with the tip of one finger.

Nick peered at her display.

'I took over from Rowena with the other camera—before the lady knocked it to the floor, exposing the film.'

'Yes, but these Polaroids are all taken in the shed—before the trunk was moved. You took more in the hospital room and left them to dry on the bench, remember?'

Nick looked upset.

'You're right—then I ran out of film. I must have left them there,' he said. 'I'd better go over and get them.'

'You could check on the fuel gauge of the car at the same time,' Sarah suggested, but before they could go anywhere the door opened and Mary-Ellen burst into the room.

CHAPTER NINE

'PAUL PAGE is missing!' Mary-Ellen fired the words at Nick, then scowled at Sarah and Rowena.

'D-didn't B-Barry see you?' Nick stammered. 'He was going to call on you, but his baby was arriving and then— Have you been in? Been at the motel?'

'I'm not staying at the motel. Paul was there, and I've been at the guest-house next door. I can't bear motels, they're so soulless. And where else would I have been but inside, in this filthy weather?' Mary-Ellen added. 'It reminds me of just how miserable our family holidays were! Why anyone would live in such a God-forsaken spot is beyond me. Unless, of course, he or she were hiding from something!'

The poison in the tip of the sentence made Rowena squirm, but Nick didn't seem to notice it. He was probably too busy wondering whether to tell the woman her detective was dead or leave the breaking of that bit of news to Barry.

'When did you last see him?' Nick asked, and Rowena silently congratulated him, although if Mary-Ellen knew he was dead she must also have guessed he'd have been found by now.

Rowena pictured her sitting in her room at the guesthouse, the tension building and building as she waited for someone to bring her the bad news. Finally, it had all got too much and she'd decided to force the issue.

'About nine or nine-thirty. We had dinner together at the motel, and talked for a while, then, although it was raining, I walked back to the guest-house because the motel dining room was overheated—they lit a fire when the power went out and the room was like an oven. I needed to cool down.'

'And this was about nine or nine-thirty?' Nick repeated the times she'd given, but made them into a question.

'About then,' Mary-Ellen told him coolly. 'Lorelle likes to lock up at ten and I was in well before that. He was going to collect me at nine-thirty this morning, after we'd both had breakfast.'

Nick glanced at his watch, though Rowena could have told him it was close to one.

'Weren't you worried earlier—when he didn't turn up?' the young policeman asked.

'Of course not. I thought he'd had an idea and gone out to investigate it. That's what I'm paying him to do. I just assumed he'd come back eventually.'

'So you last saw him at nine-thirty last night,' Nick persisted, and a sudden flash of wariness in Mary-Ellen's eyes told Rowena he'd pushed too far.

'Why are you asking?' Mary-Ellen demanded. 'What's wrong? What's happened?'

She looked at Sarah and her eyes narrowed.

'And what's *she* doing here?'

The menace in the woman's voice made Rowena shiver.

Nick looked uncomfortable, as well he might. Neither the procedures manual nor his mystery reading had prepared him for the actuality of telling a woman her friend was dead—murdered.

'Mr Page's body was discovered at the hospital this morning.'

'He died at the hospital? Was he sick? What happened? Did he have a heart attack?'

Again she turned to Sarah, addressing the final questions to her.

'I can't talk about it, but I'd suggest you wait until Barry's available and get whatever information you need from him.' Sarah spoke gently.

'Wait? What do you mean—wait?' Mary-Ellen demanded, rage staining her cheeks a vivid ugly scarlet. 'How long am I supposed to wait to find out? Why wasn't I informed immediately?'

'As Mr Page was a mainlander, the homicide squad was informed of all particulars and it's up to them to inform the next of kin,' Nick said, with more composure than Rowena would have given him credit for. 'Naturally, Barry will want to talk to you about it. About why Mr Page was here as well.'

Angry colour flared again in Mary-Ellen's cheeks.

'To find out who killed my sister, that's why he was here. Thanks to the incompetence of the local constabulary, her murder went undiscovered for four years. Do you think I'd have any confidence in you and that country clodpole of a sergeant solving the mystery?'

Nick didn't flinch from the insult. Instead, he asked the question Rowena had wanted to ask.

'But your sister's body hadn't been discovered. There was nothing to find out, no proof she had been killed, when you brought him over.'

'I *knew* she'd been killed!' Mary-Ellen spat the words at Nick. 'Knew it all along!'

Then she turned away and after a final scowl at Sarah almost flung herself out the door.

'But she shouldn't have known the body would be found,' Sarah said. 'And why am I the target of her anger? Did either of you notice? See how she glared at me?'

'Couldn't miss it,' Nick said, while a vague shadow of an idea flitted across the edges of Rowena's mind—not tangible enough to grasp but of sufficient strength to make her shiver at its unknown implications.

'Let's have lunch,' she said to Sarah. 'You can tell me about your Tony, and about James. Get our minds off murder for a while.'

Sarah looked so dubious Rowena smiled.

'We can try,' she told this woman she barely knew, but had already come to like—and, more importantly, to trust.

They'd reached the café when Sarah must have remembered what they'd been discussing before Mary-Ellen's arrival.

'No!' she said, grabbing Rowena's arm. 'You go ahead and order. *Caffè latte* and a toasted ham and tomato sandwich for me. I want to see the car and get those photos. The photos are less important, but the car thing is bugging me. I need to know if the engine was left running for any length of time.'

'Why's it worrying you?'

Sarah gave a half-smile.

'I guess because Mary-Ellen was so definite about giving herself an alibi for after ten. My initial estimate, using body temperature, would put Paul Page's death later.'

'So she could have left the heater running deliberately.'

'Or turned it on after she'd killed him. He might have questioned her turning on the engine, even to auxiliary, while they were carrying out an illegal search of someone else's car.'

'Fingerprints?' Rowena asked.

'In this weather no one would query someone wearing gloves.'

Rowena sighed.

'OK, go back and check the car, but I still don't see how we can incriminate her. And would a layperson know about the body-temperature thing? I'm a nurse and maybe if I'd thought about it I'd have figured it out, but I wouldn't have known enough to set it up.'

'Change your reading matter,' Sarah suggested. 'Anyone who's read any mystery fiction knows something about body temperature and could figure out a warm car would slow the cooling process of a body.'

As Sarah returned blithely to the police station, Rowena found herself shivering. It seemed unbelievable that anyone could plot and plan so deviously.

And why?

The motivation still nagged at her.

*   *   *

Satisfied the cool-room was cooling itself efficiently, David wiped his oily hands on a rag and turned to the policeman.

'OK if I grab some gear and pack Sarah and Rowena's things to take into town for them?'

'Of course it's OK,' Barry said gruffly. 'I've been here over two years now, and reckon I know you, mate. If you did in that wife of yours, or that fellow, I'd be very surprised, but I can muck things up for you as well if I don't do it all by the book.'

David understood what he was saying, and felt a flicker of gratitude towards the man.

They were walking back to the house, where Barry had left the police vehicle.

'So, what do you think of having a daughter?' David asked, thinking a neutral topic might ease the tension.

'You know,' Barry began, 'I was that delighted. Really over-the-top kind of excited, and relieved, because of poor Margo having to go through so much pain, but then I started thinking about all the things that can go wrong. What if she fell off the bed one day or, later, off a swing. And then there're car accidents and rapists and—'

David rested his hand on his companion's shoulder.

'Hold it right there! That's lack of sleep talking—and over-excitement. You can't go through life thinking of all the bad things—no one can. We'd all go mental. Think instead of the good things. When will she smile? Will it be at you? Or the practical things. How are you at changing nappies? You can only do the best you can for the people you love. After that, it's out of your hands.'

He was thinking of Rowena as he said it, thinking of the pain he must have caused her when she'd already suffered so much pain herself. He missed Barry's reply but guessed it was positive because the man's step became lighter and swifter, and David had to hurry to catch up.

Inside the house, however, Barry returned to policeman-mode.

'You tell me what you want, I'll pack it,' he said, as David led him towards the bedrooms.

It took longer that way, but eventually they were done.

'Have you keys for this place? I know locking it isn't a guarantee of security, but if we locked it—and the big shed—it would save me having those two fishermen out here. Save the tax-payers some money as well.'

David produced keys and handed them to Barry.

'I guess the shed keys are still over there. I've always kept it locked because I've worried about kids getting in there and possibly hurting themselves.'

They drove over to the shed, where Barry dismissed his deputies and locked the big doors.

'Weather's clearing, so we should have the homicide boys here on Monday. I'll be glad to hand it over to them, too!' he said, as they headed back to town.

'What about my car? Will it have to stay where it is until they see it?'

'Afraid so,' Barry told him. 'They'd have my skin if I moved it and destroyed evidence in the process.'

'Well, with this place off-limits and a locum to do my work, I guess I won't be needing it anyway.'

'How's the lady doctor getting around?' Barry asked.

'Hire car. Well, eventually, a hire car. I'll pay for it, of course, but I needed mine and she needed something so I arranged with Bob to hire one. She hadn't picked it up because she didn't need one while I was working with her, and since then—well, you know how things have been.'

'Grim to say the least,' Barry murmured, but then he smiled and David knew he was thinking of his baby daughter.

Birth and death—the entry and exit points in human life—both unpredictable—both, at times, with elements of violence, always with elements of pain.

For someone.

'Why did she bring him over here? What could a private detective do that a policeman couldn't?'

Barry glanced his way.

'Been wondering the same thing myself. In the long run, a private fellow can spend more time and energy on one particular case. We coppers have other things we have to do. Your wife's case—well, I doubt the file's been opened for years either here or in the city. I certainly haven't been through whatever we've got on it in our office, though I will as soon as things settle down.'

'So he came over to discover what had happened to my wife and just by chance stumbled on her body?' David scratched his head. 'Seems darned coincidental to me!'

'Me, too,' Barry agreed, 'but coincidences do happen.'

'I suppose he *was* working for Mary-Ellen. Did you check him out?'

Barry gave him an exasperated stare.

'When've I had time to check anyone out?' he demanded. 'I phoned the mainland this morning with his details and left it to someone over there to contact his business and his next of kin. Haven't been back to the office since, though I guess they'll fax me if they learn anything.'

Silence fell, but there was an uneasiness in it—explained when Barry asked, 'What exactly happened when your wife disappeared? You weren't here, were you?'

David closed his eyes as he mentally re-created those dreadful days.

'The twins came over on the ferry with the horses, then Mary-Ellen took the horse trailer back on it,' he explained. 'I flew over, as arranged, on the Wednesday flight and Sue-Ellen wasn't at the airport to meet me. I eventually phoned Ted Withers and got a lift out to the house. She wasn't there either, and when she didn't come home by seven, I phoned Mary-Ellen first to make sure she hadn't gone back to the mainland with her, then the local policeman, your predecessor.'

'And did he come out?'

'Not that night. He called around, put out a message on local radio to look out for her, but the car we kept at the house was here so, well, no one knew what to think.'

'Was she having an affair? Did you think she was off with some chap?'

David glanced at the policeman, surprised by the acuteness of his guess.

'I didn't *know* she was having an affair but, yes, it had happened before and it *is* what I thought. But when neither Mary-Ellen nor I heard from her after twenty-four hours, I began to get really worried. Mary-Ellen did as well, and it was she who rallied people to come over and help the locals search.'

'But if you weren't here when she actually disappeared, why were you the main suspect?'

David found himself smiling, although at the time there'd been no amusement in the situation.

'The presumption was that she *had* been here when I arrived, though Ted had come in with me and knew I'd looked around the house and yards and called to her. But the theory was that she'd turned up at some time, and we'd had an argument, possibly over her not meeting me at the airport. The terminal staff testified that I'd been upset when she wasn't there. You know what transport's like on the island—so I *was* angry. Naturally, the logic went that during the argument I killed her then hid her body.'

'Ted's testimony must have helped you,' Barry said, and David found himself shuddering.

'It was the only thing on my side!'

Nick was reading a fax, upside down, as it continued to spill from the machine, when Sarah walked back into the station.

'Can we get those photos and check the car now?' she asked, when he looked up then moved guiltily away from the shiny stream of paper issuing from the machine.

'I suppose so,' he replied, though he glanced back as if he'd prefer to watch the fax arrive.

'It will only take a couple of minutes,' Sarah pointed out. 'You've got the keys.'

He nodded his agreement and led her out of the room, but as he paused to put on his raincoat, more as protection against the icy wind now the rain had eased, she saw a figure standing at the door of the surgery.

'Oh, no! It looks as if I've got a patient. I'd better go,' she told him. 'You get the photos and check the temperature-control setting in the car. If it was on, it'll make a difference to the time of death and Barry will want to know as soon as he gets back.'

She walked away, then remembered Rowena.

'Sorry, Nick, but when you're done, could you call at the café and let Rowena know where I am? She can bring a sandwich and coffee back to work for me.'

'Easier said than done,' Rowena told Nick when he joined her a little later. 'Both the coffee and sandwich are already cooling fast—they'll be terrible before I get them to her.'

Nick dropped into the chair meant for Sarah and grinned at Rowena.

'How about I have these and you order more for the doctor? That way these don't go to waste, and hers'll be hot.'

He spooned sugar into the coffee as he made the suggestion, and started on the sandwich before Rowena could object.

She ordered more, to take away this time.

'So, what's happening? What did you find out? Was the heater on?'

Nick continued to eat but a slight downward movement of his head suggested assent.

'I don't suppose you checked the fuel gauge. If it was on empty we'd know the heater kept running until the fuel ran out.'

'I'd have had to turn the key on to check the gauge and Barry's got the car keys. I could see the temperature controls through the window now it's not raining so much.'

Rowena nodded, but although Sarah had been anxious to know about the heater, she didn't see what difference the time of death would make, given it had been the kind of night when no one in their right mind would have been out and about to witness nefarious deeds.

And David wouldn't accept her alibi!

Where was he now? Still out at the farm?

Being with him, the way things were, wasn't much fun, but it was worse not being with him, she decided.

'You paying for all of this?' Joan Mathers, the coffee-shop proprietor, put the paper cup of coffee and the wrapped sandwiches down on the table.

'I guess so,' Rowena told her.

'No, I'll pay for mine!' Nick objected, and he dug his hand into his pocket, pulling out first the photos he'd collected from the autopsy room, then a clatter of loose change.

'Don't be silly—it's on me,' Rowena told him. Afraid Joan might ask about the photos, she thrust a note into the woman's hand. 'Keep the change!'

Joan moved away so swiftly Rowena realised she must have grossly overpaid her, but right now tip size was irrelevant. Right now, clearing David's name was uppermost in her mind.

She flicked at the photos with one finger, idly separating them out as she thought about David, then she looked more closely.

'That's wrong,' she said, stabbing a finger at the one

showing the unclothed body stretched out on the stainless-steel table. 'Look—look at the legs. Why didn't we think of it yesterday?'

Nick peered dubiously at the photo she'd indicated.

'What about the legs?'

A gust of wind flipped the photo over, and they both turned towards the door, Rowena's heart accelerating when she realised who'd walked in.

'I was looking for Sarah,' David said. 'I've brought her things back from my place. Yours as well. I didn't want to take the liberty of going into your house so I've left them at the surgery.'

His face was so controlled she could read nothing in it—no emotion, but none of the coldness he'd been directing at her either.

'Isn't Sarah there?' Nick asked. 'She was certainly heading that way when I left her.'

'She must have been called out to someone,' Rowena suggested. 'Was my car gone?'

'I didn't look,' David said.

He hovered uneasily just inside the door, the mask slipping to reveal an uncertainty so unusual in him she ached to hold him in her arms and offer comfort—whether he wanted it or not.

Failing that, she could, once again, offer a hot drink and food.

'Here!' she said. 'Sit down and eat this sandwich. I ordered it and the coffee for Sarah but as she's gone...'

He still looked uncertain and, guessing unhappily that it was her presence holding him back, she stood up.

'I'll go back and mind the surgery. There's probably a note from Sarah somewhere on my desk, saying where she's gone and when she'll be back.'

They passed midway between the door and the table and although Rowena felt the tug of emotion this momentary closeness caused, she stifled it. It was bad enough having to accept that their passionate interlude had been nothing more than a release of tension for David, without making a fool of herself by showing her heartbreak.

There was no note from Sarah but, then, the new doctor hadn't worked with them long enough to know it was David's habit to always leave word of where he'd be. Rowena studied the appointment book, mentally working out which patients might come in this afternoon now the wild weather was easing.

Mrs Stable was unlikely to come—it would still be blowing, and possibly raining, up her end of the island, and she hated driving at the best of times. Ned Grimes was the following appointment, presumably coming to check Sarah out—well, unless she got back soon he'd be disappointed. Then—

A noise rocked the building, or had the earth shifted with whatever had caused the explosion?

Rowena dropped the book and raced outside, joining shopkeepers up and down the street.

Thick black smoke billowed up from behind the hospital. The school!

The thought had barely registered before Rowena took off, running swiftly towards the school.

David, coming from the café, fell in beside her. Nick, with longer legs, and youth on his side, streaked ahead. It seemed to Rowena as if the whole town was running, all the women converging on the cluster of buildings where the island's children between the ages of five and fifteen would be gathered—most of the men heading for the volunteer fire station where they'd break out the fire equipment. Again!

'It's on an upper storey. Perhaps the science lab in the junior high school building,' someone said as they reached the schoolyard.

Rowena felt relief thud in her heart as she saw the smaller children all being shepherded safely towards the fence. Behind them, the bigger primary kids were moving in a less orderly fashion, but still well out of the danger.

'Stay here and check the little ones for shock,' David told her, but the cries from the block beyond the primary school kept her moving. Teachers could treat shock.

The heat from the fire bit through her clothes as she came closer, and the scene, of staff and pupils staggering out of the burning building, helping others where they could, made her wince.

She whipped off her coat and wrapped it around a teenage boy whose blazer was smouldering dangerously. She sat him down and looked up in time to see David disappear into the building.

Paralysed with fear for him, she stood and watched as smoke enveloped his figure, hiding him from view. Then the cries of those who'd got out reminded her of her training and she began to function again.

'Annie, are you OK?'

The young sports mistress nodded.

'Good! How about you scoot over to the hospital and rustle up as many blankets as you can? Take a couple of pupils with you—doing something will take their minds off the shock.'

She wasn't certain if, medically, that was good or bad, but as Annie gathered a group of teenagers and they all trotted off together, she decided it couldn't be too bad. Now she moved among the onlookers, asking for coats, entrusting each person with a youngster.

'Wrap him in your coat and get him to sit down,' she explained, passing a young lad who was sobbing with either fear or relief to old Bert from the butcher's. 'Once he's settled down a bit, check him for burns—ask if he's hurting anywhere.'

'Just when we need rain, there is none,' someone muttered, and Rowena looked up to see the still gale-force wind whipping the last of the clouds from the sky.

The ambulance arrived, closely followed by the fire-engine. The volunteer fire-fighters joined school staff who were already playing water on the flames. Resolutely ignoring her need to know David was safe, Rowena continued to check the casualties, loading a lass whose asthma had been triggered by the smoke into the ambulance, then a youth with a badly burned hand.

'Get them both hooked up to oxygen then take them back to the hospital,' she told the attendant. 'Jane will have called Jackie in, and they'll do what they can until one of the doctors can get there.'

Slowly the story of what had happened came together. A chemistry experiment requiring heat and what must have been a faulty gas canister exploding.

'But all gas canisters have to be tested regularly,' she protested, as she sent a couple of students with minor burns across to the hospital by foot—their minders by their sides.

'The school ones are tested oftener than regular ones,' Annie told her, returning with blankets so helpers could retrieve their coats and wrap blankets around their charges. 'It's the kind of thing that should never happen, but maybe it was a leak from a connection.'

Her voice trembled as she spoke, alerting Rowena to her fragility.

'Sit down yourself,' she told the younger woman. 'And wrap one of those blankets around your shoulders.'

Annie slumped to the ground.

'I'm OK,' she whispered, but Rowena knew she wasn't.

She knelt down and put her arms around the trembling teacher.

'It's Shaun—he's the chemistry teacher—he'd have been right there when it went up.'

Rowena felt the pain as her heart squeezed tight. David's in there as well, she wanted to wail, but that wouldn't comfort Annie and certainly wouldn't help her own anxiety.

'Let's not think the worst just yet,' she murmured. 'Explosions are funny things. The impact might have shot him to safety, you don't know.'

A cry from the crowd made them both look up—in time to see the roof collapse onto the upper storey.

Annie's anguish escalated, and all Rowena could do was hold her tightly and hope people would think the tears streaming down her cheeks were for Annie and Shaun.

'They've got everyone out!'

The whisper went through the crowd like a prayer, confirmation coming from Darlene, the headmistress of the junior high school, who had been ticking off staff and pupils from a roll.

'Shaun's unconscious but David thinks he'll be all right,' Darlene added, squatting down beside Annie and relieving Rowena's anxiety at the same time.

'Will you stay with Annie?' she asked Darlene. Once assured, she set off herself, seeking the man she loved.

Needing to see for herself that he was all right.

He was bent over a stretcher at the back of the ambulance, helping the attendant find a vein for a catheter for Shaun. On a second stretcher, the slight form of a badly burned young lad made Rowena wince.

As if sensing her presence, David looked up, and a white smile flashed in the sooty blackness of his face.

'Can you go over to the hospital? Call the mainland and ask for an air ambulance to airlift these two out. Tell them there could be as many as four to go. It's going to depend what we find when we start looking more closely at the injuries. Check the latest wind speed before you phone so you can let emergency services know. I doubt one will be able to land before morning, but we've got to try.'

'I'll go across there in a minute,' Rowena told him. 'Right after I've checked you out.'

Her voice defied him to argue, but he shook his head and said, 'I've a few minor burns, love, that's all. I grabbed a hose before I went in and doused myself. Wet wool might smoulder but it doesn't burn too easily.'

Love! He called me love!

The word sang in Rowena's heart as she headed for the hospital, detouring via the back of the police station to check the wind speed on the display box of the computerised weather station.

It was probably stress, she warned the bits of herself which were celebrating this miracle. It didn't mean anything!

But the warmth of pleasure persisted, so even the news that a plane wouldn't be able to land on the island's windswept strip before morning failed to dim her happiness.

'We'll manage,' she said to Jane, who was trying to work out how many beds they could rustle up if some of the minor burns and shock cases needed to be kept in overnight.

'Maybe!' Jane replied. 'And only till tomorrow if the people David's bringing in need one-to-one attention.'

David!

'What can I do—where do you want me to start?' Rowena asked, ignoring the warmth the mention of his name had caused and focussing solely on the immediate crisis.

'With the group on the front veranda, if you could,' Jane suggested. 'First- and second-degree burns on arms and hands. I've set up buckets and basins of water out there and have them all soaking their burns, but I haven't had time to really classify the injuries. There's a jug of a glucose drink I made up and glasses there as well—make them all drink. And if you take some dry dressings and cover anything that needs covering, those that are OK can go home.'

Rowena made her way out to the veranda where seven students were laughing and joking as they dunked their arms in the water.

'You lot look like malingerers,' she told them. 'Let's see what we've got.'

As she worked her way down the line, drying the area around the burns, wrapping wounds in dry gauze, she pieced together the story of the explosion. The experiment had been set up in what was supposedly a fire- and shock-resistant chimney but perhaps a blockage in the chimney had blown the flames outward instead of sucking them upward. Most of the pupils burnt had been injured trying to pull the teacher, who'd been knocked unconscious by the explosion, away from the flames, or by tentative attempts to douse the fire.

Rowena suspected a lot of the levity in their description of the event was the result of shock, and was glad to see parents arriving from all over the island. She'd warn those with injured children to watch for delayed reactions.

'You're Toby Warren, aren't you?' she asked the quietest of the group, right at the end of the line.

'That's right,' he murmured, carefully cradling his injured wrist in his good hand.

The pale skin was an angry red, and the burn spread around his arm like a wide bracelet.

'My shirtsleeve caught on fire but I didn't know,' he explained.

'I think we'd better have the doctor take a look at this,' Rowena said gently. 'The rest of you, stay here until one of your parents turns up to take you home and tell whoever it is I want to see them before they go.'

The teenagers all nodded. She acted as school nurse when required and also gave them relationship lectures, so they were willing to accept her as an authority figure.

'Come on, Toby. Inside with you.'

The lad was shivering and Rowena grabbed a discarded blanket to wrap around his shoulders.

Jackie was in the single ward, bent over the young asthmatic.

'If you want a bed, try the outpatients room. Jane's set up some temporary accommodation in there.'

Rowena led Toby through the ward, past the casualty room where David, with a white coat over his sooty trousers, was bent over Shaun Riley, and into the outpatients room, now fitted out with hastily put-together beds.

'I hate to think how musty some of these mattresses must be,' the aide in charge muttered to her as she waved Rowena and the new patient to a spare bed in the corner.

Rowena sat Toby on the bed, then went in search of a drink for him. With the body's defences all marshalled to fight the effects of the burn, fluid depletion was a real threat.

Once he was settled, she walked through to Casualty where David and Jane were now working on the badly injured student.

'Tell me what to do while you go and have a shower,' she told David. 'You're hardly sterile and that's of prime importance in burns.'

He looked up at her as if bemused to hear someone giving orders, then his eyes gleamed momentarily and he smiled.

'Perhaps some day soon things will return to normal and I can tell you why I got Sarah over here in the first place. There are sterile, treated dressings in those packs—just put them over the burned areas. Don't attempt to peel off any clothing that's stuck to skin.'

Rowena nodded, too delighted by the smile—the gleam—to do more. Then she remembered Toby.

'I put a lad with burns right around his wrist in Outpatients—you might take a look at it on your way.'

'Of course,' David said, then he looked around as if puzzled by what—or whom—he saw. 'Did you find Sarah? The entire island population has heard about the fire, so how come she's not here?'

'She may be at the surgery. She could have been driving

back from somewhere and missed the excitement so doesn't know what's happened.'

David seemed to accept this explanation, for he departed, promising to be back within minutes. Rowena donned a coat and gloves and began unpacking dressings to lay across the burns.

'Once this is done, we'll make you more comfortable,' she told the teenager, though she guessed the pain relief, dripping into his veins with the fluid, was already having that effect.

Rowena and Jane worked steadily, knowing they lacked facilities to do more than stabilise the patients and hopefully keep the wounds free of infection. Shaun Riley remained unconscious, X-rays showing a hairline fracture of his skull but so far no sign of a haematoma developing.

'It's a matter of watching everyone,' David told them when all patients had been transferred to beds and the senior staff were grabbing a quick meal in the kitchen. 'We've only a limited number of monitoring devices so it's back to basics. We need to check blood oxygen levels, fluid levels, any change in respiratory patterns, and with the younger ones treat any rise in temperature immediately. Post-burn seizures are common in children.'

'Where's your locum? Sarah?'

It was Jackie who asked the question which had flitted through Rowena's mind from time to time as she'd moved among the patients.

Now, hearing it asked aloud, fear gripped her and she felt her muscles tense.

David frowned and looked around as if expecting Sarah to appear, but it was Barry who entered the kitchen. The policeman had made an attempt to clean up, but sooty marks marred his uniform and a black streak showed where he'd run grimy hands through his fair hair.

He also looked exhausted and was frowning ferociously—as if daring another catastrophe to occur.

'How are things here?' he asked Jane. 'You got everything under control?'

Jane assured him they were handling it and Barry turned his attention to David.

'Where's your lady doctor—Sarah?' he demanded, as if David might be secreting her somewhere about his person.

'We were just wondering that. Why?'

'Because I've had her husband on the phone, wanting to know why he can't contact her—or anyone else for that matter.'

'Sarah went on a call,' Rowena said uncertainly. 'Nick might know. He was the last to see her.'

'How did she go?' Barry asked, then he turned to David again. 'Did you get that hire car?'

David shook his head.

'Not yet.'

'Then she didn't take that, and your car's where it was and Rowena's car is behind the surgery. How did she go?'

Rowena's fearful tension turned to nausea and she saw David's face pale as he repeated Barry's words.

'How did she go?'

CHAPTER TEN

'WHERE'S Mary-Ellen?' David asked the policeman when no one answered the question which had echoed hollowly around the kitchen.

'I haven't checked but I assume she's at the guest-house,' Barry said. 'Why?'

David realised how many people were waiting for an answer, and knew he couldn't voice his totally unfounded suspicions.

'She's probably the only other stranger on the island at the moment so would be the least likely to have heard of the fire. I thought she and Sarah might have been together...'

Fear and tiredness weighed down his shoulders as he paced the room, trying to work out what could have happened.

'Nick saw Sarah go—where's he?' Rowena asked, the huskiness of her voice revealing her hidden terrors.

David moved closer to her, aching to take her in his arms and assure her everything would be all right. But who was he to be making such assurances, and how could he hold her when his gut instinct told him he'd be putting her in danger if he revealed how he felt?

'I'll ask him, and put out a radio call,' Barry said. 'It's dark outside so we can't do much till daybreak, but if you hear anything at all, let me know. That chap's going to be phoning all night long.'

'Well, at least I won't have to worry about being tried for murder,' David muttered to Rowena. 'That chap, as Barry calls Sarah's Tony, will kill me if anything's happened to her.'

Rowena's fingers clasped his arm, tightening on his muscle as if to hold him back from danger, and a warmth he shouldn't have been considering right now swept through him.

'Rowena!' He murmured her name with a helplessness he'd never felt before, as fear and frustration were overcome by a need to explain.

A tiny glimmer of light lit the clear beauty of her eyes, and a tremulous smile wavered uncertainly on her lips. And suddenly, in the hospital kitchen, amid staff and chaos, with his wife dead, his best friend missing and a murder charge hanging over his head, David knew for certain he'd fallen in love again. That what he felt for Rowena went deeper than desire, deeper than anything he'd ever felt before—or ever imagined he *could* feel again.

'Let's go back to work,' she said quietly. 'Do what we can, and forget about the other things for a while.'

'I'm going to roster people through the night so we've staff capable of functioning tomorrow if we can't fly out the worst cases.'

Jackie's voice broke through the fragile web of magic, which the suggestion of a smile had woven, and David dug deep, summoning up reserves of professionalism, blotting out both love and fear.

'Jane's already gone off duty, and the junior and one aide will go off at ten.'

She looked enquiringly at David.

'Are you and Rowena prepared to stay? I think you'll be playing nurse rather than doctoring, but we need the extra hands.'

'Of course we'll stay.' David answered for Rowena as well and once again, through all the concerns eating away at him, came the warmth he now associated with all his thoughts of her.

But when Barry returned at midnight to report that no

one had seen or heard from Sarah, nothing could take away the cold certainty that something evil had befallen her.

'All Nick saw was a figure in an oilskin waiting by the door of the surgery.'

'And where was Mary-Ellen at the time? Have you asked her that?'

Barry lifted his heavy shoulders in a weary shrug.

'She drove out to the farm for a picnic lunch, she says. Wanted to see the old place once again before she leaves.'

'She's leaving? You're letting her go? And how? How can she leave?'

'Special charter flight tomorrow morning. It will come in after the air ambulance. Sarah's husband's coming over on it. A couple of homicide detectives as well, so they'll interview the lady at the airport and it will be up to them to decide whether or not she can leave.'

Barry paused.

'I've no reason to suggest they keep her here,' he added. 'None at all! And they'll warn her about letting them know where to find her on the mainland.'

There was another, longer pause then Barry asked, 'Why don't you trust her?'

Rowena had joined them by the door of the main ward, and David sensed support in her presence.

'I don't know.' He spoke slowly, trying to put formless impressions into words. 'It's as if I hadn't known her at all—or perhaps she turned into another person when Sue-Ellen disappeared... As if she'd taken on her sister's persona in some kind of ghostly—ghastly—transformation.

'Because she is her sister,' Rowena whispered, her eyes dark with a horror David couldn't understand. She turned to Barry and clasped his arm. 'The photos—where are the photos Nick took? Nick and I were looking at them in the café, on the table, then David came in and I went back to the surgery. Get the photos from Nick.'

She made an order of the words then spun away, crossing

the ward to where Jackie leant over Shaun Riley, taking a quarter-hourly observation of the man's vital signs.

Barry muttered something about crazy women and departed while David watched the whispered conversation between the two women. Then Rowena walked away, heading for the office, the agitation so evident in her steps that David followed.

'What is it? What's wrong?'

Rowena turned towards him, dark-lashed eyes huge in her ash-white face. She shook her head as if words were now beyond her, but as he stepped towards her she held up her hand.

'Go back to work, David. There are patients who need you in there.'

He hesitated but in the end he obeyed, and Rowena, seeing the weariness and defeat in the slump of his shoulders, knew she'd killed the fragile bud of whatever it was that had sparked between them earlier.

But it had to die, she told herself. If her worst fears proved true, then David, being the man he was, would stand by his—

Wife!

The word crashed through her head, shattering her dreams. And here she was, seeking the proof which would destroy her own happiness.

The keys to the storeroom were in the drawer Jackie had indicated, but though the door unlocked easily the smell of musty paper suggested it wasn't opened often.

Filed by year, Jackie had said. Well, that was easy to work out as Rowena had been seven the year she'd broken her leg. Midsummer and she'd been jumping off the high rocks at the beach to show her brothers she could do it.

Back then, the old *Trusty* had serviced the island weekly, so minor accidents had been treated at the hospital. Old Sister Caine had set her leg, joking about the practice she'd had that summer because one of the Merlyn twins, over at their grandfather's for the holidays, had broken her leg two days earlier.

'You'll be company for each other in hospital,' Sister had said, but Sue-Ellen—and Rowena was certain it *had* been Sue-Ellen but she had to see the file for confirmation—had preferred the company of the nurses and aides, preferred being petted and spoilt and told how beautiful she was.

'So the body should have had an old break in her right leg?' Barry muttered when he returned to find the old file open on the desk and Rowena waiting for him beside it. 'Could you see that in a photo?'

'I don't know,' Rowena said crossly, 'but I'm pretty sure you can see if a bone *hasn't* been broken. I know I didn't get a good look at the photo, but my impression was that it was undamaged.'

She shifted impatiently.

'Have you got them—the photos?'

Barry shook his head.

'Sorry! Nick's out searching for Sarah. I contacted him on the two-way but the reception's so bad I couldn't make him understand what we wanted. He probably has the photos on him.'

'The woman we thought was Mary-Ellen smashed the camera Nick was using in that room. Did she remember the broken leg and want to destroy the evidence of the unbroken one?' Rowena thought for a moment, then contradicted herself. 'No, that can't be right—the real autopsy will reveal it if the bone's unbroken.'

'Yes, but once the body's off the island, who'll ask? I mean, someone'll send me an autopsy report but under the circumstances I wouldn't have shown it to David. Even supposing he knew she'd had a broken leg in her childhood.'

'Who'd had a broken leg?' David asked, appearing suddenly in the doorway. He didn't wait for a reply but looked at Rowena. 'Can you come? I'm going to operate on Toby's wrist, open up the skin because the swelling's blocking circulation to his hand.'

'Did Sue-Ellen ever mention breaking her leg?' Barry asked him, and David looked puzzled, then glanced at Rowena.

'You think—*No!*'

He shook his head, pain settling like a huge weight on his shoulders. 'She had a scar, a small one, on her right leg, midway between ankle and knee, but I don't remember her telling me how she got it. And it was so small, you'd barely notice it.'

He looked from one to the other.

'It won't matter, you know. All the skin would be so desiccated you wouldn't be able to tell.'

'But you could see a mend in a bone,' Rowena reminded him.

'Or the scar on the skin of a woman still alive,' Barry murmured.

Rowena walked towards the door, her own disappointment and fear enough of a burden to bear.

'Get the photos, Barry,' she said. 'And keep hold of them. Just in case.'

He didn't ask in case of what—didn't need to.

And David didn't ask either but, what with Sarah missing and the possibility his wife might still be alive, he was probably beyond rational thought.

At seven next morning, when staff sent home to sleep the previous evening were returning to relieve those on duty, a call came through from Bob Forster, a farmer at the far western end of the island. He needed an ambulance for a woman he'd found collapsed in his dairy.

'A woman with red-gold hair?' David demanded when Jane relayed the message.

'I didn't ask, but how many women are missing? It has

to be Sarah,' she said. 'Barry's on his way out there. Bob called him first.'

She studied him then added, 'I know it's no use telling you to go and get some sleep. You'll want to be here when she's brought in—but at least go into the kitchen and have a solid meal. Rowena, you take him, and see he eats something. It sounds like Sarah will be out of action for a while, and we'll need one functioning doctor.'

David turned towards Rowena. She was pale with tiredness, and seemed diminished in some way. As if the night had stolen her last reserves of strength. The need to hold her—to comfort her—was almost overwhelming, but he knew his desire to tell her how he felt—to make plans and promises—would be impossible if Sue-Ellen was alive.

Then he stepped towards her anyway. Damn it all! The relationship he'd dreamed of might be impossible but they were still friends. He put his arm around her and walked with her towards the kitchen, feeling the long lines of her body, the swell of her hip, as they moved together.

The closeness made him think of all the might-have-beens and suddenly he realised too much had been left unsaid. Walking past the kitchen door, he steered her out onto the veranda where he turned her so he could look into her face.

'I love you, you know,' he told her, keeping his tone conversationally light. 'That's why I asked Sarah to come over, so I could clear up all the mess of Sue-Ellen's disappearance—divorce her or have her declared dead, whichever the legal people thought appropriate—and start a new life with you. Courting you!'

Rowena didn't reply immediately, studying him instead, perhaps reading the truth of his words in his eyes.

'I know that now,' she murmured, before adding despairingly, 'For all the good it will do us!'

He lifted his shoulders in a helpless shrug, then nodded because she was right. Rowena knew him well. He wouldn't, couldn't, abandon Sue-Ellen right now, no matter what she'd done.

As for leaving Rowena? Would such a thing be possible?

He groaned and reached out for her, drawing her into his arms and holding her close, and then, with all the love and desperation in his heart, he kissed her.

The approaching wail of the ambulance siren broke them apart. Rowena stepped away from him, reaching out for the veranda railing for support.

'You go and see to her. I'll come in shortly,' she said, in her cool nurse-receptionist voice.

It was tantamount to goodbye and David had to accept it, merely touching her lightly on the shoulder in the hope physical contact might convey the myriad emotions he couldn't voice.

Sarah was conscious—and vocal.

'Barry told me Tony's on his way. I've got to get out of here, David. I need to have a bath and clean up and look normal or he'll go berserk.'

In spite of his pain, David found himself smiling at this reaction from the woman who was weakly struggling to detach a fluid line from her wrist.

'Normal's going to be hard when you've a bruise the size of a fist on your cheek. Do you want to talk about it?'

Sarah shuddered.

'I've told Barry what happened. Talk about stupid. As soon as I saw who it was at the surgery door—saw it was Mary-Ellen—I should have walked away.'

'You're a doctor, you couldn't walk away from a possible patient. But you must have gone with her in her vehicle—why?'

Sarah's smile started off brave but wavered slightly as the fearful memories shook her.

'She had a gun, stupid! Of course I went with her. In fact, I drove.'

'Another gun?'

His disbelief was obvious.

'Ask Barry,' Sarah said, her voice weak with exhaustion.

'Later,' he assured her. 'Right now, I want to get you settled. You need to rest. There'll be no question of you going out to the airport if you don't rest now.'

David finished his examination. He couldn't bear to think what his wife had done to this woman he counted as his best friend. For the moment, it was enough that Sarah was safe.

'The air ambulance is coming in first, then the charter flight. I'll check the times with Barry. I'll have to go out to the airport with the patients, but someone will bring you out in time for the second plane.'

'The fire—I didn't even ask!' Sarah said. 'How terrible. The ambulancemen said it started with a chemistry experiment. Were there chemical burns as well?'

Knowing his patient wouldn't obey his orders to rest until she had details, he explained what had happened.

'The school will bring in experts, of course, but apparently it was caused by a blocked chimney and a leaky gas fitting. A combination that was as unlikely as it was volatile.'

Rowena came in as he finished and, sensing her quiet presence, he turned to her.

'I want to check on the patients we're sending to the mainland. Will you stay with Sarah?'

'Of course,' she said.

But seeing the two of them together made David uneasy. He'd been carefully protecting Rowena, but it seems Sarah had been the one in danger. If Mary-Ellen was indeed Sue-Ellen, could her jealousy of a woman she'd never met have lasted all this time?

The fact that Sue-Ellen hadn't loved him—well, not solely him—made her possible jealousy of Sarah seem even more unreasonable.

Unreasonable, or something more sinister? Psychotic?

And if the woman—whether Sue-Ellen or Mary-Ellen—was mentally unstable, was Sarah safe even now?

David felt as if his head were being squeezed in a vice. He had to check on the patients they were airlifting out, but he needed to talk to Barry as well. A quick phone call…

Duty won. There were too many checks to be made before transporting seriously injured patients for him to deny them the time. He'd have to leave whichever twin it was to Barry and Nick.

'Barry can't find her,' Nick told him when the younger policeman came across to let them know the air ambulance was on time and would be landing in fifteen minutes. 'He's had to go out to the airport to meet the homicide chaps. You'll see him out there.'

'I'll go out in the ambulance. Will you take Sarah out to meet her husband off the second flight?' David asked him. 'She shouldn't go but you can't stop a woman when she's made up her mind, so I'd like someone to keep an eye on her.'

Nick agreed, but when they all met up at the airport later, after the ambulance flight had departed and the small charter plane was approaching the runway, David realised Sarah had two minders. Rowena was also there. He ushered them inside and insisted they sit down.

The Range Rover arrived last, pulling up as the plane taxied first away from the small terminal building then turned to come back. Ignoring the parking area behind the small terminal building, the woman at the wheel of the earthbound vehicle drove around to the front, closer to where the plane would eventually stop.

Barry approached the vehicle with caution, but Mary-Ellen—or Sue-Ellen—seemed unperturbed. David followed the policeman, aware that Nick was behind him, providing back-up for his boss.

'I've some questions to ask you about what happened yesterday,' Barry said to her.

'Yesterday?' the woman said. 'You mean the fire at the school? Nothing to do with me at all.'

'I mean taking Dr Kemp at gunpoint out to the National Park. I'm talking about charges of deprivation of liberty and attempted murder.'

Barry, who must have been exhausted after two sleepless nights, was making no effort to hide his anger or lower his voice.

Even from a distance, David saw the woman's face blanch.

'You can't know that. She's...'

Was she going to say 'dead'?

If so, she stopped herself in time.

'She's lying to try to save her precious lover. Setting me up to take the blame. My sister's body is found on his property, the gun that shot Paul Page is found in his pocket—what more proof do you want?'

Barry stepped a little closer.

'And as for this ridiculous accusation about taking her anywhere,' the raging woman continued. 'You can't prove a thing! It would be my word against hers.'

She was so unperturbed that even David began to wonder if Sarah had been mistaken.

'I can prove you're not who you say you are!' Barry told her. 'You're not Mary-Ellen whatever-it-is, although you've been living under her name—under false pretences—since your sister disappeared.'

Sue-Ellen—David accepted now that it *was* his wife—paused in the act of pulling a canvas carryall out of the vehicle. Her eyes narrowed as she looked at Barry.

'What would you have done if your husband had murdered your sister by mistake?' she hissed. 'Of course I pretended to be Mary-Ellen. As long as he thought he'd killed me I was safe.'

'Safe to spend your sister's money!' Barry retorted. 'There will be fraud charges laid against you as well. Paul

Page was investigating *you*, not your sister's death, and he emailed reports to his office on a daily basis. Some of the information his office has is very interesting.'

Something in Barry's voice suggested to David that this might not be entirely true, but Sue-Ellen obviously didn't catch the nuance. A hand gun, small but deadly-looking, appeared in her hand.

But Barry appeared unflustered by it—perhaps because the plane had now stopped and a group of men had disembarked and were approaching Sue-Ellen from behind.

'As for Dr Kemp's story, I'm sure a fingerprint check of the vehicle you've been driving will prove who's telling the truth.'

'Yes, I made sure I put my hands on as many unlikely surfaces as possible.'

Sarah had come up behind them and now stood beside Barry, facing her tormentor.

Sue-Ellen gave a cry of rage and aimed the gun directly at her.

'You're out of bullets, remember?' Sarah said. 'You fired the last of them at me as I tumbled down the cliff. Again and again until all I could hear was the click of an empty chamber.'

A bullet zinged past David's ear.

'Get down!' he yelled, and as Barry dragged Sarah to the ground he flung himself at Rowena, hurling her to the tarmac.

But Sue-Ellen had stopped shooting. She was racing towards the plane, the gun now levelled at the incoming policemen who'd dropped down behind a refuelling tanker.

'If I hit that the whole place will go up,' she yelled. 'You'll all die!'

She made it to the plane and scrambled aboard, firing wildly towards the pilot, who'd been the last to leave so was still closest to it.

'Can she fly?' Barry asked.

David nodded, but he doubted whether she had any intention of flying anywhere. The twin engines roared to life and the plane raced up the runway then, without lifting more than a foot off the ground, continued straight out over the cliff and into the sea.

CHAPTER ELEVEN

'WELL, for a holiday that started out with disaster, it didn't turn out too badly,' Tony Kemp announced.

He was standing with his arm around his wife's shoulders on the wide stone patio in front of the Witherses' house. Ted had invited them all to a lunchtime feast to celebrate the news that he and Kelly were, years after they'd given up all hope of having a family, expecting a baby. It had been a joyous explanation for Kelly's distraction, confirmed when Ted had persuaded her to see Sarah professionally.

Barry and Margo were there, demonstrating what life was like after an addition to the family. James was inside, sleeping off a morning playing with new lambs. Lucy was flirting light-heartedly with Nick, and Rowena and David were sitting quietly on the wide stone balustrade, holding hands and saying very little.

Sarah looked around the people who'd become her friends, then focussed on the one who'd always been close to her.

'I guess our next visit will be for a wedding,' she said. 'Have you finally got around to asking Rowena to marry you? Or are you still dithering about what people will think? Or whether you're finally cleared of all suspicion? Or whatever other dread you're nurturing? Honestly, David, for someone who was once so positive about life, you sure had the stuffing knocked out of you by that woman!'

David grinned at her, then kissed Rowena.

'We'll do things in our own way, thank you, Dr Bossy! You concentrate on your own problems, like persuading

Bessie Jenkins to give up her job at the tuckshop until she's cleared of hepatitis.'

Sarah smiled smugly. 'It's done and, no, I won't tell you how I did it. A woman needs some secrets.'

'Speaking of secrets, I've had copies of the lab report and also a final summing-up of things from the homicide people.' Barry addressed the gathering at large, but David knew the words were directed at him.

'You know, of course, that the fingerprints on the underside of the seat in the Range Rover proved that Sarah had indeed been in it, and bullets gathered on the cliff where Sarah fell proved someone had been shooting out there. But the lab report's even more interesting. By sheer chance, some of the dust I vacuumed up under the chest in your shed had oats in it.'

'Oats?' Rowena echoed faintly. 'What do oats have to do with anything?'

'Horses eat oats,' Barry explained. 'Generally, after such a long time, it would be hard to positively tell one kind of grass-eating animal's manure from another, unless the animal had been on a specific diet. The oats suggested the animal had been hand-fed, and the Merlyn twins' horses on the mainland were stabled and fed oats.'

'I don't see where all this is leading,' Ted Withers complained. 'Does anyone else understand?'

Sarah smiled at him.

'I think I do,' she said. 'One of the problems all along has been where the body was when the police searched David's property and, presumably, his place in Melbourne. The twins brought two horses over, and Sue-Ellen—though everyone thought it was Mary-Ellen—took the float back. The trunk, with the body in it, must have been in the float, collecting a bit of horse manure on the bottom of it. I bet later, after the island property had been searched, she said she couldn't leave the horses there unattended, and brought the float back for them.'

'Yes, she did,' David remembered, 'but I can't see her lugging the trunk around on her own. It's impossible.'

'When we went back to the shed we found a lightweight trolley—a wheeled thing the old man probably used to shift his heavy collectibles around the shed.' Barry took up the explanations again. 'The original interview with the chaps on the boat the day she went back to the mainland mentioned a trolley in the float. They assumed it was used to shift bales of hay because there was hay in there as well.'

'Or a trunk cleverly disguised as a bale of hay!' Rowena suggested.

Barry nodded at her.

'Where she kept the trailer while the mainland search went on is anyone's guess, but if it was near stables, the smell could have gone unnoticed.'

'Or been contained by the trunk to a certain degree,' Tony put in. 'There are documented cases of bodies left for years in left-luggage facilities at railway stations. Obviously the smell didn't attract too much attention.'

'Anyway,' Barry continued, 'once she had it back on the island, she was safe. It was a year before David decided to come and live in the house, and by then she was off spending her sister's money and, no doubt, felt she'd got away with murder.'

'So why come back at all?' Rowena asked. 'Why open up the investigation? Why take the risk?'

'I wasn't lying when I said Paul Page had been investigating her,' Barry responded. 'Though I only had the fax telling me that the morning the planes came in. Apparently she'd gone through all Mary-Ellen's money, so when one of Mary-Ellen's ex-husbands died she sued his estate for a share. His family didn't think Mary-Ellen would have behaved that way—they'd always liked her and hadn't blamed her for leaving the old man who'd been a bit of a tartar. Anyway, they hired a firm of private detectives to check her out and Paul Page's firm got the Australian end of the investigation.'

'But had he any proof she wasn't who she said she was?' Rowena asked. 'And why was he with her, pretending to be *her* detective?'

'They were both too clever by half,' Barry replied. 'As soon as she realised he was snooping around, she turned the tables by going to his firm and asking specifically for him to help her find her sister's murderer. Once David mentioned he was going to clear out the shed, chances were the body would come to light. What better idea than for her to discover it? No doubt she thought it would throw Paul off the scent. Of course, *he* saw it as an opportunity to get close to her and find out more.'

'So when she suggested they look in my car for something, he'd have fallen in with her plan?' David tightened his arm around Rowena as he made the suggestion. They'd come so close to losing this magical love before they'd properly explored it, and he felt his heart juddering at the memory.

'Actually, she told me about it as we drove out to the National Park,' Sarah said. 'I think she wanted me to know how clever she was. Paul Page had already shown her he wasn't going to let her out of his sight, so she told him she'd arranged to meet David in his car, knowing Paul would come, too. She let Paul sit in the front passenger seat, saying there was more room there for his legs, and being behind him made it easier to produce the gun without him suspecting. Later, she got into the driver's seat and turned on the engine and the heater, then, by pure chance, as she was driving the Range Rover back to the motel, she saw David dash across the street from the hospital. She waited until he'd gone inside, then went across and slipped the gun into the pocket of his raincoat.'

'I guess, having visited since childhood, she knew everyone left their rain gear in the outer porch,' Ted put in.

'But once you found that gun, where did the other gun come from?' Margo asked her husband. 'Why was she wandering around with two guns?'

'They were a pair. Mary-Ellen had lived abroad and, according to information Paul Page had collected, one of her husbands had given her a gun and shown her how to shoot. Prior to her return to Australia, she'd bought a second gun for her sister. No doubt, she suggested the island would be an ideal place for Sue-Ellen to learn to shoot, so they brought the guns over with them.'

'Then she was killed with one of them!' David murmured, the enormity of the crime still weighing him down.

'Exactly,' Barry agreed. 'In fact, she told Sarah a lot of that as well, though the information remained hearsay until we proved what we could of it. She wasn't experienced with firearms so she couldn't shoot anyone from a distance, but she boasted to Sarah about daring her sister to try to fit into the trunk. Apparently the story of their mother having a trunk of old clothes was true, and in their childhood they'd hidden in it. Mary-Ellen had gone along with the dare, making it easy for Sue-Ellen to shoot her and hide the body at the same time. The bullet hole in the bottom was filled with debris, and wasn't found until the trunk went to the lab.'

'But she brought the guns back to the island this time, five years later,' Rowena said. 'Did she intend to kill someone all along?'

'I'd say so.' It was Tony who made this assessment. 'I saw some of Paul Page's reports and he was getting far too close to the truth. He'd even found a record of a sale of the second anklet so presumably, like the hair-dye thing, Sue-Ellen had insisted on buying an anklet for her sister to complete the double image. When she realised Paul Page knew more than he should, the decision to get rid of him, while irrational to us, no doubt seemed logical to her. And, having killed once on the island, it might have seemed easier to repeat it over here.'

'Well, I like that explanation better than doing it here to deliberately target me as chief suspect,' David said. 'Though I think revenge—or perhaps jealousy—ran through all of Sue-Ellen's behaviour. Things were often "unfair" to her, beginning, I suspect, with Mary-Ellen going first through the birth canal. And there was an instability there as well.'

He sighed then looked at Tony.

'I owe you a huge apology for putting Sarah in danger. From the moment Sue-Ellen arrived, I sensed a threat but, seeing her as Mary-Ellen, I felt she might object to me replacing her sister with another woman. Naturally, I thought the target would be Rowena, and did my best to deflect danger from her. But Sue-Ellen, though she'd never met Sarah, had always been jealous of my friendship with her. She didn't know Sarah had remarried so when I contacted who I thought was Mary-Ellen, telling her I had Sarah coming over to the island as a locum to give me time to clear the sheds, she could have leapt to the conclusion I was considering remarriage and assumed I had Sarah as the likely candidate for a bride.'

Rowena saw Tony's arm tighten around his wife and knew the security of that kind of protection. She could almost feel the love flowing between the couple—between the other couples here as well—and understood it was her own new and different experience of it heightening her senses.

Then Sarah shook her head.

'She was definitely irrational. Frighteningly so. I tried to talk to her, to get her to explain. But in all she said—raved, really—I still couldn't get an answer to why she killed her sister.'

'Money!' David said. 'And in the end it's what brought her down, don't you see? First she went through her own inheritance from her parents. A lot of the problems in our marriage were money-related. I worked sessions at the Childrens' Hospital on a voluntary basis and Sue-Ellen felt it was a waste of good earning time. She hated me doing it and nagged incessantly about it. Taunted me about my "charity"!'

'Money!' Sarah murmured. 'How often it comes back to that.'

David nodded, then, as if he needed to explain, added, 'Looking back from this different perspective, I can understand her behaviour towards me after she'd killed her sister. She was in such a towering rage but knowing now that it was Sue, I can see she was blaming *me* for what she'd done. Killing her sister would have been like killing part of herself, and in her mind it was all my fault because I couldn't provide her with the money she wanted—or perhaps needed.'

He smiled, but the expression held little mirth. 'It's strange, but the wrangling over money, the unhappiness it caused, must have stayed with me. When I gave up paediatrics—came here to the island—it was a relief to get away from the money-oriented side of specialising. I realised later it was an underlying motivation in making that decision.'

'Not to mention getting away from colleagues who viewed you with suspicion,' Rowena, who'd heard so much of his story in the last few days, reminded him.

'Yes, but getting back to Sue-Ellen,' David said. 'It must have seemed unfair to her that Mary-Ellen was not only free of encumbrances in the way of a husband, but was inordinately wealthy to boot. She killed her sister to get her money, went through it all, then greed prompted her to try for more from the ex-husband's estate. I think Tony's right in saying she considered herself safe, killing on the island. Then it became a bit of a game. By inveigling Paul to accompany her to my car, she also implicated me, and getting rid of Sarah just added a bit of spice to her delight.'

Rowena felt the cold presence of evil brush against her skin and shivered in the warm sun. But David's warmth sustained her, promising safe harbour—eventually.

'But she didn't get rid of me,' Sarah reminded them. 'As soon as we stopped, I got out and ran. OK, so I ran over the edge of a cliff in sheer fright when she fired at me, but that turned out to be my salvation. When I didn't move, she fired the rest of her bullets in my general direction, then assumed I was dead and eventually went away. But that's all in the past. Let's look to the future. When are you two getting married?'

Sarah had brought the conversation back to where it had begun. Rowena felt David shift as if in discomfort, and understood his hesitancy. As far as she was concerned, it was enough to know that he loved her as deeply as she loved him. Marriage could wait.

'We'll do it one day,' she told Sarah. 'But quietly. Just the two of us and whatever officials the law deems necessary.'

'I'd marry her tomorrow if she'd agree to it,' David said, 'but we'd both be uncomfortable. There's so much to be sorted out, and Sue-Ellen was my wife, whatever else she was. I guess it's an element of respect I'm talking about.'

'Good grief, David,' Ted exploded. 'You must be the only man in the world who'd even think of showing respect for a murderer.'

Rowena felt David flinch and she nestled closer to him, taking his hand and clasping it in hers.

'We don't need marriage vows to prove anything either to others or ourselves,' she said firmly. 'We've already pledged our love to each other, and for now that's enough. And David's right. Whatever else Sue-Ellen was, she was a fellow human being—a woman he once loved very deeply. For that reason alone, he needs time to mourn her—

to mourn the original Sue-Ellen, not the sick woman she became.'

David's fingers tightened on hers but it wasn't until he was driving her home that he spoke.

'You are without doubt the most remarkable female ever put on earth,' he said, as casually as if commenting on the weather.

Rowena hid her twinge of delight and denied the compliment.

'No! You are!' he repeated. 'You not only stood by me right through this nightmare, even when I was hateful and hurtful to you, but you're now putting into words things I can barely sort out in my head, let alone explain.'

'I know how you feel, that's why,' she said, leaning over so she could rest her head on his shoulder. 'When I first realised I was thinking of you as a man—feeling an attraction towards you—I was almost overcome with guilt. I felt as bad as if Peter had still been alive and I was betraying him by considering you that way.'

David nodded and she knew he understood. It was one of the wonderful things about David—he understood so much. He'd understood she'd had to tell Peter and Adrian about him, and had walked with her to the lookout on the cliff-top, where she'd always felt closest to them, and had waited by the gate while she'd communed with their spirits.

He understood that though they might spend part of every night together, delighting in the joyous journey of discovery that was physical love, the conservative islanders preferred that they each woke up in their own beds, so one or other of them was usually commuting home in the early hours of the morning.

And would be until they were finally married.

'It's rather nice,' David said, as he stopped the car outside her gate and turned to take her in his arms. 'This courtship thing! I know I long for the day when I'll wake with your warm body curled against me, but at the same time the meeting and parting does heighten the senses, and add spice to our love-life. Perhaps, after all, we have something for which we can thank Sue-Ellen.'

Rowena tasted the kiss he pressed on her lips, and felt the flutters of excitement it generated shimmy through her body. And, as ever when David kissed her, she had a sense of coming home. Of finding safe harbour after a long and dangerous voyage.

Modern Romance™
...seduction and
passion guaranteed

Tender Romance™
...love affairs that
last a lifetime

Sensual Romance™
...sassy, sexy and
seductive

Blaze
...sultry days and
steamy nights

Medical Romance™
...medical drama on
the pulse

Historical Romance™
...rich, vivid and
passionate

29 new titles every month.

*With all kinds of Romance for
every kind of mood...*

MILLS & BOON®
Makes any time special™

MAT4

MILLS & BOON

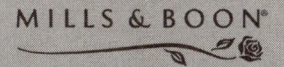

Medical Romance™

A WOMAN WORTH WAITING FOR
by Meredith Webber

Dr Detective – Down Under

After five years Ginny is still the beautiful, caring woman Max remembers, and a wonderful emergency nurse. But she clearly hasn't forgiven him. It takes a murder investigation to bring them together, and in their new-found closeness, Max knows that he'd wait for this woman for ever…

A NURSE'S COURAGE *by Jessica Matthews*

Part 3 of Nurses Who Dare

ER nurse Rachel Wyman has come back to Hooper to think about a new career. But Nick Sheridan adores Rachel, he needs her – and so does Hooper General Hospital. He's determined to help Rachel conquer her fears about nursing, and win her love, but does she have the courage to take them both on?

THE GREEK SURGEON *by Margaret Barker*

Sister Demelza Tregarron found herself hoping against hope that Dr Nick Capodistrias and his young son could be the family she'd longed for. In Nick's arms the life she had dreamed about seemed within reach. But when his ex-wife reappeared, Demelza feared she was about to lose those she loved…all over again.

On sale 5th April 2002

Available at most branches of WH Smith, Tesco, Martins, Borders, Eason, Sainsbury's and most good paperback bookshops.

MILLS & BOON

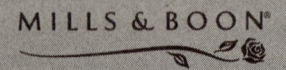

Medical Romance™

DOCTOR IN NEED by Margaret O'Neill

Nurse Fiona McFie was damned if she was going to let Tom Cameron walk all over her – and the uneasy attraction that simmered between them made her want to fight him even more. But Tom proved to be a talented doctor and a devoted father, and soon Fiona realised that all she really wanted was to give Tom and his children all the love they could ever need!

TEMPTING DR TEMPLETON by Judy Campbell

A 'bonding' course certainly isn't Dr Rosie Loveday's idea of fun – until she meets her gorgeous instructor, Dr Andy Templeton. Their mutual sparks of attraction are impossible to ignore, but Rosie is determined to stay single. It's up to Andy to persuade her otherwise and he's got the *perfect* plan!

MOTHER ON CALL by Jean Evans

Even though it meant juggling single motherhood with a new job, Beth moved to Cornwall so that she could start being a GP again. Then an embarrassing encounter with Sam Armstrong, the new senior partner, marked the beginning of a tense working relationship, made worse by the chemistry they shared. Sooner or later something – or someone – would have to give...

On sale 5th April 2002

Available at most branches of WH Smith, Tesco, Martins, Borders, Eason, Sainsbury's and most good paperback bookshops.

Treat yourself this Mother's Day to the ultimate indulgence

3 brand new romance novels and a box of chocolates

= *only* £7.99

Available from 15th February

*Available at most branches of WH Smith,
Tesco, Martins, Borders, Eason, Sainsbury's
and most good paperback bookshops.*

MIRANDA LEE
Secrets & Sins
revealed

SEDUCED BY HER BODYGUARD AND STALKED BY A STRANGER...

Available from 15th March 2002

*Available at most branches of WH Smith,
Tesco, Martins, Borders, Eason, Sainsbury's
and most good paperback bookshops.*

Starting Over

Another chance at love...
Found where least expected

PENNY JORDAN

Published 15th February

Available at most branches of WH Smith, Tesco, Martins, Borders, Eason, Sainsbury's and most good paperback bookshops.

FREE

2 BOOKS
AND A SURPRISE GIFT!

We would like to take this opportunity to thank you for reading this Mills & Boon® book by offering you the chance to take TWO more specially selected titles from the Medical Romance™ series absolutely FREE! We're also making this offer to introduce you to the benefits of the Reader Service™—

- ★ FREE home delivery
- ★ FREE monthly Newsletter
- ★ FREE gifts and competitions
- ★ Exclusive Reader Service discount
- ★ Books available before they're in the shops

Accepting these FREE books and gift places you under no obligation to buy; you may cancel at any time, even after receiving your free shipment. Simply complete your details below and return the entire page to the address below. **You don't even need a stamp!**

YES! Please send me 2 free Medical Romance books and a surprise gift. I understand that unless you hear from me, I will receive 4 superb new titles every month for just £2.55 each, postage and packing free. I am under no obligation to purchase any books and may cancel my subscription at any time. The free books and gift will be mine to keep in any case.

M2ZEC

Ms/Mrs/Miss/Mr ....Initials ....

BLOCK CAPITALS PLEASE

Surname ....

Address ....

....

....Postcode ....

Send this whole page to:
UK: FREEPOST CN81, Croydon, CR9 3WZ
EIRE: PO Box 4546, Kilcock, County Kildare (stamp required)

Offer valid in UK and Eire only and not available to current Reader Service subscribers to this series. We reserve the right to refuse an application and applicants must be aged 18 years or over. Only one application per household. Terms and prices subject to change without notice. Offer expires 30th June 2002. As a result of this application, you may receive offers from other carefully selected companies. If you would prefer not to share in this opportunity please write to The Data Manager at the address above.

Mills & Boon® is a registered trademark owned by Harlequin Mills & Boon Limited.
Medical Romance™ is being used as a trademark.